An End to Chivalry

A Short Novel
and
Five Stories

An End to Chivalry

A Short Novel
and
Five Stories

by

TOM COLE

An Atlantic Monthly Press Book

LITTLE, BROWN AND COMPANY · BOSTON · TORONTO

LIBRARY OF CONGRESS CATALOG CARD NO. 65-20744

FIRST EDITION

The author wishes to thank Alfred A. Knopf, Inc., for
permission to quote five lines of John Crowe Ransom's
poem "Man Without Sense of Direction" from his SELECTED
POEMS; and the *Atlantic* for permission to reprint stories
which originally appeared in its pages.

ATLANTIC-LITTLE, BROWN BOOKS
ARE PUBLISHED BY
LITTLE, BROWN AND COMPANY
IN ASSOCIATION WITH
THE ATLANTIC MONTHLY PRESS

Published simultaneously in Canada
by Little, Brown & Company (Canada) Limited

PRINTED IN THE UNITED STATES OF AMERICA

To Ellen

Contents

I

An End to Chivalry

The weather continues inexpressibly fine. Today was spent, unfortunately, amid the follies of Carnival time.

— *from Goethe's travel journal*

Prologue

THE courtship of Howard Hawthorn and Sarah Dashner was set against the collegiate impedimenta of pens and notes and papers, and they wrote their differences there: Sarah was left-handed and Howard right-handed, formidably right-handed, keeping notebooks and journals in a regular script that marched month after month across the yellow legal pages in impeccable and blotless lines. Although Sarah never quite lost the feeling that there was something in his rectitude that entirely missed the point, neither did she ever lose the guilty respect that the left hand can feel for the right. Her own handwriting constantly changed size and shape. She took her infrequent course notes on paper napkins. She got ink on her fingers when she wrote, and she wrote in that utterly unreformed left-handed manner: namely, backwards, with her wrist tucked under, and her elbow pointed out.

Yet they had their likenesses. Both were tall; both wore loose sweaters; both were blond (although Howard's hair seemed white under the sun, while hers was of a heavy honeyed color that could seem almost dark).

On the campus of their small, high-minded college in Pennsylvania, Sarah already felt jaded, thought of herself as one of those loony, lazy ex-prodigies who come to nothing. In high school, near Chicago, she had been precocious and agile, inspired a protest circle of herself and the two other girls who considered themselves intellectuals and who reveled with her in being called the Three Freaks and quoted at each other in senior year, "There will be time to murder and create." Now she majored in French literature, wrote essays full of cynical and amusing non sequiturs on *Adolphe* and *Liaisons Dangereuses,* consumed an incredible amount of yoghurt, and listened to music from the hi-fi.

Howard was slow-moving, calm, accepting honors as they came. He had for so long excelled in the measurable worlds of youth — field and classroom — that it seemed in the nature of things. He played football as varsity end and, in fact, team captain, but only out of obligation to the college: his true love was mountains — climbing alone one summer in the Rockies, skiing alone one summer in Chile, escaping alone to New Hampshire or the Adirondacks whenever he could during the school year.

He majored at first in classics, but uneasy among the poets, he turned to history, which he absorbed with gigantic appetite for memorization. A shrewd instructor observed that his approach to Greek history was much the same as to a summer chain of mountains: what he wanted was to wander off into it, alone. Yet the high-minded college made its mark on him. He decided to become a lawyer, a Good Lawyer concerned with the poor, and then if he proved worthy, a Judge and Preceptor to his republic; and to be with Sarah as lover, husband, and father to her witty children.

When he told her of his plans, she laughed. "You don't want me. You want mountains."

"I want both," he said.

He wanted to come down from peaks and high winds to find her near a fire, the light warm on her hair while she read French novels. The room would be high-ceilinged, paneled in dark wood, with the firelight playing across tiers of books in old leather, many of their titles in Greek; and somewhere else, altogether elsewhere, his achievements would already be acclaimed.

Sarah had her doubts. When they had first begun to talk, on afternoons of golden November smoke, he walking beside her with the self-conscious roll and hitch of the over-sized athlete, she had enjoyed needling him. "Howard, your trouble is, you've won too many elections. You've been given too many gold-plated effigies. You lack humility." How skillful. Howard's pride was all in his efforts to be humble. Yet he enjoyed laughing at himself (as long as he knew she was going to be his): "I *am* a gold-plated effigy," he said. "It's uncomfortable as hell."

When he forced five-pound books on classic sculpture upon her, she said she finally saw how he got that way: he had been made by one of "the lesser Roman imitators" of Polyclitus. Also true, he admitted. She liked to peek at his letters from home, which arrived every morning like fan mail (correspondence with her own Glencoe homestead consisted of a monthly phone call, collect), and she finally found out where he hid his journals, which she read — enthralled at his thrashings, at the spiritual roll-and-hitch that made even his sentences uneasy. At last she couldn't know whether to laugh, deride, deflate, scorn, or to be touched. Amazing herself, she chose to be touched. There was something about all that momentum, the zeal, the struggles, the escaping into mountains. When he was off skiing (head of pale floss flying against New England snow) she could not keep his body out of her mind, and when the impulse still came to resist the momentum in him, she found herself saying, *Why bother?*

They went off dancing; they made love; they married. After graduation, he thought it best to dispose of military service, to be a pilot. "I can see it now," said Sarah, "the story of our lives. *She* wanted a nice dirty room in Paris, but *he* dreamed only of going into orbit."

For three years she watched the jets: long white plumes, brilliant against the sky even when the Texas ground had been blotted in dusty sunset. She gossiped with the "idiot wives," ate more yoghurt, read more novels, had an occasional headache, cooked from a French cookbook, and fended off the pilots who were grounded on the days when Howard flew. He kept in shape by running at dawn, by racquet games at dusk, and when the officers in Bachelors' Quarters went off, as they said, to hunt pussy, he went home to read Toynbee. Or he and Sarah went off dancing. Or they made love. But as months passed, Howard fell more and more into fits of abstractedness, in private, sometimes in public, until Sarah knocked on his forehead as a front door, or called him on an imaginary telephone. "Hello? Anybody home . . . ?"

His pale hair was thinning at the temples when he was to be discharged, and he was ready, anxious to travel. But now Sarah wasn't so sure. There was law school still to come, and they wanted to begin a family, and then there would be clerking, junior humiliations — when was adulthood supposed to begin? Howard nodded gravely. The race was getting keener, he admitted; it was only the swiftest American youths who could end their adolescence before social security set in. But still, to travel, to find a sense of measure . . . and he spoke glowingly, not of nice dirty rooms in Paris, but of Herodotus, who had gone to Egypt and even beyond the Black Sea, and of other such lore that struck her as delightful and irrelevant, with the result that

they flopped down on their living room carpet like children with the funny papers, poring over an atlas map of
the Mediterranean, the sea a bright blue, the land green,
except for mountains. To the left, she made smudges on
France and Italy with a ballpoint pen; to the right, he
traced out Greece, the Cyclades, the Sporades with the fine
line of his mechanical pencil. They had a bout of simultane-
ous discourse; from her — color, music, wine, silk blouses,
umbrella pines, artichokes, fountains, Botticelli, Venice,
Easter, oranges, late coffee, sunshine, people — while he
spoke of things high and simple and classic, of sonorous
names that ended in -*cles* and -*tus*. It was the year before
family and work should become all, and their smudgings
and tracings converged at last upon one place — Sicily —
where they thought they could find abundances of what
they both wanted.

1

In Rome they were rushed. In Paestum, alas, it rained.
Then they were amid the great dry march of hills across
the center of Sicily.

Early February; Sicilian spring, therefore, and as their
train chugged around sunny corners the valleys poured
down to them a froth of almond blossoms. Prickly pears
flew past their windows, and olives, cypresses, and above
them on precarious juttings of land mass the towns clung
like tortured rooks. It was a quiet train on a workday
morning. Only three quick-eyed young Palermitans shared
their compartment, on the way to celebrate a friend's wedding on one of those coiled hilltops deep in the interior.
"A poor and hopeless place" these city men were going to
visit, but they passed wine to the Americans, exchanged
laughter and platitudes, guarded the creases of their dark
suits, and then left them — Howard and Sarah, peaceful,
sharing an orange from a tree of the land through which
they were rolling, and both hoping that their arrival among
the temples of the southern shore was to bring them at last
something Greek, a mood of the Mediterranean, something
of the ancient sun they had come so far to seek.

By late afternoon, it seemed so. The sea below them
carried blazons of sunlight as easily as it had carried the
Phoenician, the Carthaginian, the Greek, the Arab ships in
the past. Howard lectured as they stood high in the warm

wind among the sandstone temples, as they strolled along
the once sacred ridge of Agrigento. It had been the Greek
Akragas, a city of luxury and disaster, grown rich on its
good soil and the sale of pillows made by its slaves. Pam-
pering its daughters with golden tombs for their songbirds,
it had gone down in fire with the wine still on its breath —
and justly so, in Howard's notions, for it had never been
strenuous and eloquent like Athens itself. But the warmth
of what it had left amazed them both, the scarred and fluted
yellow stone, the tranquil columns and entablatures set
against slopes of green spring rolling down to the sea.
There were farms beneath them with upturned squares of
earth dark and moist as chocolate, and the orchards sweep-
ing wave on wave of blossoms so that the sea breeze was
touched with almond, and their senses, unaccustomed, sur-
rendered to the riot of that feminine, thronging spring.

The almonds were out, as advertised, but not "pinkish"
or "rose" as in the travel brochures. Sarah had discovered
that each petal had only a bright red lip at the conjugation
of the blossom and otherwise was white, nor was the white
a blankness as of paper, but a living glow, curved and
shadowed. Then the olive trees among them, time-twisted,
silver-leaved. Oh, she was glad they were there; Howard
had been right; she could never have dreamed such a spell
of blossom, wind, and sea; it was spring in the sixth week
of the year and they were facing Africa and her husband
finally seemed to feel himself at home measured against the
most whole of classic temples, whose columns now, toward
day's end, slowly turned bronze.

On that ridge there was also considerable interest in the
two new columns, which had arrived just that day, finely
sweatered, with floss hair and honey hair blowing in the

breeze, and both shaped true and tall. For the height of Sarah's body, although it put her head easily to rest now against Howard's shoulder, was such that the dark-eyed Sicilian sightseers, clustering where she walked, had to look up to take in all of her.

Curious long-tailed birds bubbled the air about the temples. Howard put his hand in a fluting — the sandstone worn by twenty-five centuries of sea winds and today warm against his palm — and asked the nearer of their chance companions what it was like to live amid . . . all this . . . all year. His name was Pietro and he was young, slight, liquid-eyed, soft in speech. He answered that he hated it. *"Pochi, pochi divertimenti,"* he said — there were no amusements except the movies, a few festivals, the chance to buy or sell a small car. There was not enough work, no chance to advance even if you worked like an animal. The people were tense, jealous, nosy, and generally low types. In his twenty-two years he had never been out of Sicily. He was always bored, always restless. Even Rome or Torino wouldn't be so bad, but his dream, he confided, leaning close with the burden of his idea, was to go to America. Near New York he had "some relatives" whose call to join them in that terrestrial paradise called Brocolino he was awaiting any month.

"Any *what*? Any century." This was Salvatore, expert motor salvager, older than his friend Pietro, and stronger, laconic, with muscular hands and neck, and — a wonder — pale eyes. Still, he said that if things were different he himself ought to go to America, where he could take a decent girl on his arm without getting engaged. "You know, the boys here get engaged only out of boredom. When there is absolutely nothing else to do." Salvatore, unlike frail

Pietro, took care to use schoolroom Italian with the tall arrivals. "Not because they have finally chosen the finest girl available, as you do in America" (gesture of tribute toward Sarah, modest smile from her), "but they are bored, the movies only change twice a week, and there you are — it's done. Then they are tied."

"*Sì, sì,*" Pietro piped in, confiding again —there was no divorce in Italy. And anything backward in Italy was twice backward in Sicily.

Nor would pale-eyed Salvatore be unhappy in the New World independently earning a sack of money. When he pronounced that solemn word — *soldi* — he rubbed his stubby fingers together and flashed a conspirator's smile.

"I, on the other hand, care nothing for money," retorted Pietro. "Life itself interests me, and here there is none."

A league of smiles from his elders, to hear late on a blossoming afternoon such pronouncements.

"Cretin," said Salvatore. "Without money we are asses with sacks on our backs. Twitching our ears. Am I right, Pietro? Admit it."

The boy cast down his liquid eyes and kicked at a Doric column. (Hadn't Salvatore lent him a few lire that very afternoon to buy coffee for the Americans?)

"Am I not right?" persisted Salvatore, to Howard now. "Do me the pleasure of telling him. He never listens to me because he knows I'm always right. He just wants to be beautiful."

"Well, it helps," Howard said, shrugging his high sweatered shoulders. "But money isn't everything, not even in America. Not even in Brocolino." Howard was troubled. He wanted to be a courteous guest, and alert, but he was torn between the ancient, silent Greeks whose memories he had sought and the new Sicilians who, talking away, had sought him. The Greeks were winning. (Shadows crept from the tall stones down the grass of the valley and then from the valleys out toward the sea. He thought of the eighty golden springs here between glory and death, nine great temples, followed by two and a half thousand years of how many decayings and humiliations . . . ?) "No," he repeated, "money isn't everything."

Salvatore made a solemn face at him and tugged with forefinger at the corner of his eye, pulling down the skin to show the moist, red part. A living mask, to say, "I have much eye. I'll not be easily fooled." Everyone laughed. He threw his powerful arm around Pietro, almost bending him in two. "Don't worry, Pietro"— his words were softening and slurring as he became more relaxed —"don't preoccupy yourself with it. I'll make a fortune and adopt you. Then you can find life."

"Okay, Turridu." Turridu was the local nickname for Salvatore. "Okay" turned out to be a fifth, perhaps, of Pietro's English vocabulary, remembered from the war. The rest was partly scatological, partly worse. "But it would go better if they found two nice American girls for us. We'll marry, emigrate, get divorced the first day in New York, if they want. But they always love us Sicilians because we are so hot." He said this without affectation. "But if you please," he added, "make them have hair of honey like *la signora*. And also *simpatica*, like her."

Sarah gave a bright smile to both boys. Then all attended to the sun's going down. Donkey bells sounded; the end of a workday. The sea seemed closer. The breeze had died and the heads of trees hung in stillness. Across the water, upon the old temple stones, across the even older hill-

sides, pale hazes of rose and saffron stretched. Howard
wanted to communicate what he felt to his wife, to these
lively boys. *"Bello,"* was all he could get himself to
say.

Salvatore spoke. "We know that you foreigners find these
ruins beautiful. But to us they say nothing. We grew up
with them. Part of the countryside, which is pleasant,
especially right now. Nothing more."

Pietro wanted to qualify, but Howard said, carefully,
"Still, you realize that we have no antiquity at home.
That's why we find this so important. We need this. We
have only the new."

"With us, instead, everything is old," Salvatore answered.

"Except the coffee machines," said Sarah.

They agreed.

"And the Alfa Romeo."

"Who can afford an Alfa Romeo?" Both young men tried
to explain that a few shiny gadgets made no difference. To
live for a while in New York, in *atmosfera moderna* with
some dancing and an envelope with eighty dollars every
week, they would exchange sun, mountains, old stones —
everything. A few pinpoints of light had appeared in the
far declivities, and one or two in the sky. The four new
friends squeezed into Salvatore's tiny station wagon — his
Topolino, "Mickey Mouse car," his "sardine can with
internal combustion"— and they drove off past the fading
almond trees. Prickly pears, which the boys called India
figs, showed their spiny cactus paddles as the road wound
close to the stone hilltop where the town lay coiled.

They were going to visit Polifemo. It was the boys' idea,
that the Americans might be entertained by him, their
Polifemo, the one-eyed brute, getting his last cosmetic

touches this evening. In three days he was to be the star of their neighborhood's float for the Festival.

"Oh yes, the Festival!" said Sarah, excited.

"Ah yes, the Festival," said Howard.

2

IT was the Festival that had crammed all four of them into one mouse car. When Howard and Sarah had arrived at the Agrigento station that morning — with the interior hills still massive in their imaginations — the baggage master had grinned and asked whether they had reserved rooms in town. It would be interesting to know this, he said, because there were no rooms in town. No rooms at the Belvedere, nor at the Hotel of the Temples, nor at the Hotel Jolly. Not even any non-jolly rooms. He was pleased with his bilingual joke.

Hadn't they seen the almond trees? In three days would be the Festival of the Almonds, and Carnival was exceptionally early this year — the same time, in fact. Half of Europe was coming down, rooms reserved in advance, "to revive the pagan sentiments." Shall we go back to Palermo? asked Howard. Shall we go back to Illinois? asked Sarah. But certainly not, the baggagemaster said; he had thought they were Germans. For such attractive people there would always be room. They could even stay at his place, except . . . and he held up his hands. And some cousins were also coming. But he would check their bags for nothing while they went to see his brother-in-law, the policeman on duty three blocks down, in town. But first they must have coffee in the station bar. The baggagemaster paid, over their protests.

They set out into the town's Arab-narrow streets, buzzing with Vespas and Fiats, plodding with red-plumed donkeys. A hard morning wind scattered sunlight and palm tree shadows brilliantly across the faces and concrete of the new square, beyond which they saw the sea-gleam a few miles to the south, and framed against it, across the tossing valley of almond trees, the toylike columned temples along their ridge.

The brother-in-law policeman wore white gloves which he wielded in spirals above his head. He blew his whistle and blew it again at the cars, busses, cycles, scooters, and donkey carts, keeping his profile and red stripes toward the audience. Along the wall and against the shops his friends were occupied in watching him direct traffic. They cheered his white fingers, they cheered his whistle, they jeered his mock rages. For the blond Americans, perhaps especially for the female, he stopped traffic in all directions.

Honking, braying, ringing, cheering.

Pay no heed to the population, he said; they are all barbarians. Yes, he knew a lady who rented private rooms in a great state of cleanliness. His friend the bus driver, at this moment located in the cafe across the way, would lead them. Find the fattest person in the cafe — that would be he. Would that he himself could offer them a coffee or brandy now, but he had his accursed work — and he spread his immaculate white gloves to them, smiled a miracle of white young teeth. He saluted, sending the square into riotous applause, except for the various drivers, who were calling him a buffoon, a mangy butterfly, a cuckolded trombone, a striped fragment of merd.

Eyes followed Howard and Sarah to the cafe, somewhat unsubtly measuring the length of her legs. Normal havoc rearose in the square. Sarah was flushed as they found the fattest man in the cafe, Howard amused and alert.

The bus driver's eyes dwindled into the rolls of his smile, for he did know that one room was free. Very tiny, but clean; many degrees higher than the street. He wished he could do more, yet it was good that they had arrived for the Festival. They would come to his Carnival party two nights hence; he wouldn't consider a refusal. The more, the merrier, and what was traveling if you could not share a few moments with the people? Family and friends, dancing, wine — he recommended his party to them, puffing them up a steep alley now, his face glistening, and sharp eyes from the fronts of shops and trattorias studying the newcomers. He learned that Howard had been in the military, was interested in history — but, the same was true of him! Such stories he could tell them, if time and the *signora* could only allow. Without a break, from 'thirty-three to 'forty-three he had served, with two years in occupation of Abyssinia. There, as an Italian, as a European, one felt isolated from all human society. The Negroes were like stinking animals, poverty-ruined; how could one even tell them apart? Yet this was so only at first, because time passed and contrasted the bright from the stupid, the comely from the ugly, but all of them had nothing, nothing, absolutely nothing. The soldiers had only to give the girls a bit of bread, a half-glass of wine, and the poor creatures were willing to do the most terrible things for them. "One did as one wished," he sighed; even men who had once been conventional. Ah, war, war, he had seen what it does to people.

The room was the size of a third-class cabin on a Turkish ship, but in a newish concrete house at the very top of town, so that the hills marched straight off from

the outside staircase in back, and one window in front
looked past the havoc of a half-built street toward the
town's tight core. The bus driver beat the price down, told
the proprietress that these were special friends, opened the
window to reduce the smell of new paint, and notified them
that he would send his nephew down to pick them up at
the temples before sunset. He wouldn't hear of objections;
the boy had a car, was very practical, and had a young
friend, also a mechanic, who lived for meeting foreigners.
That poor little Pietro, he had the temperament of an
angel but also such a violent desire to "escape" from Agrigento, as Howard and Sarah were to learn not very long
after Salvatore's Topolino rattled down to rescue them
from meditations and spring privacy at the temples.

3

THEY rattled through the steep town toward dusk, with the ignition turned off on downhill streets to save gas, with Howard's chin squeezed between his knees, and Pietro craning around to tell them how long it was since he had had a car to repair and that his friend Salvatore was only able to keep this one running because he was a genius. But Salvatore was still amused to have such human beings in such a car. "Owda is almost as big as Polifemo." "Owda" and "Sara" had been settled upon as phonetic devices for the American names. All had enjoyed singing "Che Sarà, Sarà"—"What Will Be, Will Be"— earlier on the ride, but now Pietro gazed at them with silent softened awe and twilight in his eyes as Turridu chuckled, his eyes hidden in front, for he was passing a donkey cart on a downhill blind curve with the gas turned off.

In pale aromatic dusk the Cyclops's eye in the middle of his forehead shone, harsh, with the same red that coats Sicilian carts. It was still wet; bulbous nose and Carnival leer were also fresh. Below, around the hay wagon that held his twenty-foot torso, dancers with thin pipe, tambourines, guitar, and oompa-oompa bass jug were practicing their tarantella for the Festival, looking as if they might have been self-conscious half an hour before, but now clapping at each other, whirling, laughing. Some of the girls were in peasant costume, with ribbons flowing and rainbow

skirts. On the ladder a man in gray business suit was de-
lineating Polifemo's pectoral muscles in yellow paint. They
were again on the back edge of town, but below the street
where Howard and Sarah would have to squeeze into their
room for the night. Just down the rutted alley was Salvatore's repair shop, too dark to show now. Through a gap in
the wall behind the stone sheds began the long retreat of
hills toward the north. Thicker, cooler shadows fell; a
donkey began to howl in the middle of the tarantella, and
in the distance behind the wall sheep were making stupid
sounds. "Our neighborhood," said Salvatore, his eyes pale
with self-mockery. "And Polifemo, our local hero. He built
that heavy wall."

"Also," said Pietro, "he knocked the holes in it."

Howard politely refused the invitation to meet the boys
and girls when their dance was over. He thought Sarah
perhaps was feeling a bit tired after the day.

"Not tired," she whispered. "Just weird."

Older people were gathering after work to watch. The
young dancers stamped and whirled, the bass jug continuo
blew faster and faster. Not quite breaking his gray-suited
composure, the artist bellowed, "Stop shaking the ladder!
Vermin!" and he asked someone to flick on the lights of his
Fiat, which he had aimed up the incline.

Garish, grotesque was Polifemo's red-eyed leer in the
glare of the headlights, which darkened the sky around
him. Yet his chest and shoulders and waist with all their
yellow sausage muscles kept the ancient proportions, as
Howard remarked while they drove off — but only to himself.

4

CIAO, *ciao, bambina* . . . Just one kiss more . . ." The jukebox was blaring, the metal machines gleaming, steam blasting into cups, fuchsia walls echoing, every dark head weaving with the music beat, eyes in a crooning glaze. There were rounds of laughter fired from one table to another, bright striped shirts and torso-molded dark jackets, shoes and hair in a black gloss, and only one woman in the room —namely, Sarah, with her high head still windblown and her sweater no longer feeling athletic and innocent to her skin, her eyes cast down. Madonna. Howard spooned sugar into her miniature bitter cup, whispered that they had certainly come a long way now. Salvatore and Pietro pretended not to care that they were still in their stained workshirts, not to be impressed that they sat in the middle of the blare with two blond monuments. Salvatore had fished out of his pocket a black beret, which he wore now cocked at an angle against the world. Pietro was trying to sit in the laps of both Americans at once. ". . . *oo baggiangor'* . . ." the room sang, and, "Like a tale, love passes. It was once, now is no more . . ." Howard ambled off to bring the tray of sweets back to their table. Through a scrim of confusions, Sarah remembered that he hadn't walked that way, with roll and hitch of shoulders, since college football days when he thought all eyes were on him. Perhaps it was the return of khakies, sneakers, loose sweater upon the muscles. When he put before them the tray heaped with volutes of pistachio, scarlet marzipan, vermilion plaques, his own skin was flushed a pale rose.

"I guess I do look like Polifemo to your friends. They're laughing at me." He had an Illinois accent in Italian.

"Friends. Huh!" said mild Pietro, surveying the cafe with nausea.

"No," Salvatore said. "They would give anything to look like you. They're laughing to show off to Sara. And because you left her alone with us."

With a glittering knife he set about to quarter the sweets.

Sarah said, "You mean it's still true, what everybody in the north says about Sicily?"

Salvatore held up the knife. "Revenge? The dagger? Ah, no. In the hills, it may be. But not in the towns."

"*Beh*, Turridu, why try to hide it? All the world knows we're tense and jealous."

"Well, somewhat primitive, perhaps," Salvatore said. He gave Howard and Sarah a clear look. "We just can't be tranquil where girls are concerned. Not like you others. You trust each other, treat women as human beings . . ."

"You're civilized," Pietro broke in. "Different. Civilized!"

The Americans both laughed. "I don't remember that we're all that civilized about girls. Do you, Sarah?"

"Howard's a brute," she said, chewing a scroll of bright green sugar.

"No, no, no," Salvatore insisted. "You mean it as a joke. But when anyone just looks at my sister with . . . those eyes, my blood boils. I lose all judgment." He shook his head.

"You love your sister so much?" asked Sarah.

"Not at all. I have five, and only one is not a complete cretin. But . . ."

The jukebox was turned up even louder, blasting as if under steam. "Marina, Marina, Marina, Don't leave me, Don't ruin me . . ." Rocking heads. Eyes centered on them, brash.

Sarah said, "I feel we must be a spy ring."

Pietro appealed to both. "You see why I want to get out of here?"

Howard waved his cup. "You have things here you'd miss. Things nobody else has."

"Donkeys. Foreigners always admire our donkeys."

"No. I don't mean donkeys."

Salvatore nudged Howard's hand. "You'll find trying to talk sense to him a waste of energy." His nails were oil-marked, the ends of his fingers rough; Howard's knuckles were huge and clean.

"What happens if girls come down here by themselves?" Sarah asked.

"Trouble."

The boys graphically explained.

Howard had softly hitched and rolled over to the zinc-bright counter, where he placed a thousand-lire bill, gave a nod of courtesy. The boy, in starched white, eyed him impishly, hummed, "One o'clock, two o'clock, three o'clock rock," let the bill lie.

Pietro came up in a scurry to pay.

"Thanks a thousand," the counter boy said, and handed Howard's bill back to him.

"You are a guest in our country," Pietro said. "You pay nothing."

"Nothing!" emphasized Salvatore. "Don't worry, don't

worry. When we come to America you'll have to support us
for years."

"Lucky Luciano," said Pietro, pointing at his friend.

Who took a mock swing at him, then added, "And we'll
expect that free course from you while you're here, Owda."

"What course?"

"Professor of Civilization."

All eyes followed the four out into the street, and
"Rock, Rock, Around the Clock" followed them down the
street. Moonlight. Shuttered shops. Fresh wind, with scent
of cypress or almond or sea. Immeasurable night over the
valleys beyond the town.

Salvatore drove for their baggage. Pietro accompanied
them toward their place, in a crescendo of babble. Salvatore
rattled up to announce that he had decided to take a three-
day holiday from work, to attend to their needs. Pietro
thanked God that he himself was unemployed, and would
also attend. Many offers and gratitudes. Howard saying:
Oh don't bother to come for us in the morning. Let's meet
at the temples after noon. We always sleep late and tomorrow we'll be tired.

Lies. Howard was a riser with the sun, particularly near
hills and sea, as now. And he never lied. Sarah was amused
with him. Perhaps a season here would be just the thing to
start him sleeping late, stop him reading and running at
dawn for a while, fill him with fibs and other such endear-
ing weaknesses like her own. She laughed privately through
the sequence of good-nights and wishes for golden dreams.

They were alone. It seemed an exceptional state, here.

"Do you feel squashed?" asked Sarah. "Cramped?" as
she looked for a place to drop her clothes.

Howard disliked admissions and complaints. He said no.

She pulled down her eye, Turridu style. He laughed and said yes.

Time pressed, space pressed. Archaeologically, it was magnificent here. The people had been kind. The boys had been generous, but would there never be any elbow-room or privacy?

He looked under the bed, interested to see whether a small car was waiting there to help them pull back the sheets.

"Oh God, with the sheets pulled back we'd never get rid of them."

Now, Sarah, don't be too touchy. Here was the great past, but also much they could learn about the present — customs, attitudes, thanks to the boys. And thanks to whom — baggagemaster, policeman, bus driver — did they have a room at all?

But the room. It was the Topolino of rooms. One bulb, olive- or eyeball-sized, threw a rusty wash of light. There was a sink, brand-new and tiny, but only air gasped from its faucet. Howard would make noise in the hall until they got water; Sicilians love noise and Americans love water; everybody would be happy. Long long yawn and long long stretch from Sarah: Ah no, let's just go to bed.

But the bed. It was of a size either for one American to sleep in or for two Sicilians to make love in. For two fair long Midwesterners who had spent a long day and who might have made love if they had washed — impossible. Who ever would have thought they had so many knees and elbows, and so unyielding? So they talked, huddled together, in the shadow of their suitcases. Seven years they had been lovers, had seen memorable trees, stones, effigies that day, had future children and present friends on another continent to talk about, had through a window old stars to watch, which almost paled on the edge of morning before they both fell definitely asleep.

5

EXPLOSIONS. Vespas bursting into the left ear and out the right, flatulating dynamite in transit. Trucks with wheels of stone rumbling down the middle of the bed, and the bed newly arranged of loose big paving stones. Walls doubling all sounds, ceiling resounding.

Sunlight. Golden-white, scorner of windowpanes, burner of veined eyelids.

Duet. Daughter in the hallway screaming at father, calling him a wine-soaked goat and worse, telling him to get his ugly feet out of the way so she can sweep, telling him to mind his own business or she leaves for Milano. Father shouting, Let be! Let be! You'll wake the Americans! Witch! Insignificant bitch! His voice was magnificent, able to defeat trucks and Vespas.

Solo. A protracted, descending, penetrating wail from the street below, the voice melismatic, masculine, melancholy, Oriental. He was just under their window now, a man in checked shirt, his dark face burned but not wizened, pushing his cart and singing about what was on it — cauliflowers, fine fennel, mandarin oranges, *fee-gghee-deen-deeaaa* . . .

"The walls are pretty thin," said Howard.

"Aren't they! I really hope that couple in the next room is married."

They laughed, uneasily. Puffs of air gasped from the
faucet again. Howard made as if to bellow.

"Let be, let be," she said. "You'll wake the Americans."
They put their bodies just as they were back into the
sweaters and khakies, with much jostling.

Across from them, in a ravine between houses, a great
pile of orange peels and rotting lemons had been dumped.
Yet the sun glowed upon them, and they looked redeem-
able. The sun redeemed everything — the yellowish and
whitish stones, kerchiefed heads, the cauliflowers being
haggled for amid African chantings, the frenzy of machines
and heaving sides of a brown donkey, the cart with its
red-yellow-and-orange-carved battles between Crusaders and
Saracens.

Howard and Sarah decided that it was interesting to
have sun, hot noise, Sicily, close, tight, on top of them.
For a while. They learned that the water was turned on
daily between twelve and two in the afternoon, but that
excellent baths could be had any time at the Albergo
Diurno in the center. They didn't take one, but became
famous instead at the Restaurant Giugiù by having orange
juice, ravioli, and veal à la Marsala at ten-fifteen in the
morning, for they had not eaten a meal all yesterday.

"I'm afraid the boys used up their suppertime keeping
us in sweets and sights," Sarah said.

"Also, their supper money. Today, we pay. Absolutely."

"Better yet, let's leave some money on their doorstep
and go hide."

Little girls with almond flowers in their hair played
hide-and-seek, running among the cragged trunks of olive
and drums of fallen stone. They waved white branches,

they laughed, they squealed because Festival day was coming. Shadowed, an infant goat suckled, wagging its tail like a puppy; mother goat stretched to eat branches; the tree stretched toward the high morning sun. Behind, the town rode its ridge; ahead, the Mediterranean shone, silent. Howard gave his brief lectures. Here, the court-yards of Roman colonial houses (now a paradise of dagger cacti and flowering weeds). There, against the cliff face, the sanctuary where the Sicels burrowed to get closer to the gods of earth (a thousand years before these Romans chatted on their terraces over drinks). Here, the monster temple to Olympian Zeus collapsed of its own weight be-fore it was finished, because even this old telamon — he kicked the stone giant still lying on its back with eroded face, sections slowly separating — couldn't hold it up. Dutiful, Sarah took in the hum of his voice along with the distant glaze.

The last temple standing to the east was on an immense prow of land. The land rode itself like a sea, cutting sloped green waves, splashing into blossoms. An altar here where fifty sheep could be slaughtered at once hung over the valley. Cloud shadows in puffs and pillows moved across the contours.

Sarah finally knocked on his forehead. "Anybody home?" she said.

He smiled, stopped gazing, took her to see the roseate flush marks still on a wall from the Carthaginian fires of 406 B.C. That was the end of greatness here. The color struck her. Raspberry sherbert, she suggested.

It was hard, today, to keep the antique memories of rise, balance, fall. Festival tourists were coming in droves to see the sights, and the Sicilans to see the tourists. A grave boy asked Howard and Sarah whether they already had a companion. He courteously withdrew, wishing them happiness here. An Agrigentino back home from working in the north showed them all his snapshots, mostly of himself wearing an undershirt in Belgium or smoking a pipe. They themselves were asked to pose and pose again, between the columns. They obliged, they smiled, the clouds grew thick, and by the time the Topolino rattled up, a soft rain had begun.

Pietro was wearing his black suit. Suit and boy alike seemed thin, brushed, modest, ready for graduation from something to something else. Salvatore had a clean work shirt, his black beret at an angle, and on his bony cheeks a day's growth of beard, for which he apologized — holiday. For the weather, too, they apologized. It was a disgrace. What to do? They were huddled inside the spattering tin frame.

(Howard's notion: he would like to stand bareheaded and alone in the southern rain, let time soak into him, mull.)

The boys thought they should drive to the sea, while the car still showed some signs of working. There was a beach at San Leone, but that was for fine days; perhaps tomorrow. Today they could look at the little port, Empedocle. They could have some coffee there.

"Is there much to see at the port?" Sarah asked. She sensed on her skin Howard's restlessness. They had only planned a few days here.

"Well," Pietro said. "You know, it's a port."

Salvatore: "They say a British destroyer is coming in today."

Sarah: "Perhaps we should go to the museum. It would keep us out of the rain. They say there are some fine Greek things there."

Salvatore: "Stones." But he grinned.

Pietro: "What Turridu means is that you wouldn't enjoy going with us. After the first fifty times, we stopped using it even to get out of the rain. Better to go alone, with Owda."

Salvatore: "So let's take a drive to Porto Empedocle?"

Sarah: smile. Howard: nod.

A gloom of heavy clouds moved in from the sea, sometimes bringing rain, sometimes damp gusts. Salvatore told about a freight truck that had driven into Empedocle on a wet day like this, a year ago. Just as it started down the steep approach it lost its brakes. The driver leaned on the horn, screamed, but too late — it careened out of control all the way down the narrow crowded street, killing children, goats, an old man, smashing the fine carts. People still debated whether the driver should have crashed purposely into the buildings instead, even if it meant death for him.

Now the four of them got into a discussion of crises and decisions. The boys had vivid, serious views, backed with many examples, like that truck screaming down the jammed wet street. Both Howard and Sarah felt ashamed to have mocked them in private, more so when Salvatore treated them again — to coffee and caraway biscuits — saying it was an insult even to suggest that a welcome guest pay.

Outside the coffee bar, Porto Empedocle in a windy rain seemed the scruffled, donkey-and-urchin-infested end of the earth. Grim, tight salt-and-tobacco shops, closed faces, the sea lashing and dirty, huge piles of sulphur heaped on the docks. No British destroyer. There was something about those tiers of sulphur, abandoned, uncovered in the yellow rain . . .

"Polifemo did it," said Pietro. No rest for Cyclops. The sad boy then said: to visit Empedocle in the rain is to know boredom.

They were standing in a row under the cafe awning. Howard was amused to see how much shorter Salvatore's legs were than Sarah's. He looked again, said nothing, of course.

"It's not so bad to be short," Salvatore said. "I can still get into the movies for nothing."

His powerful face, day's growth, pale eyes laughed at himself. The others laughed, too.

"I doubt it," said Howard, with his smile blond and automatic. "I sincerely doubt it."

They stood. Salvatore pushed his beret farther over one ear. He said he hadn't seen so much stuff dumped about here since the war, after the American offensive.

"Yes," Howard said. "We heard about that in the Air Force. The famous sloppiness of our Army. Dropped its garbage all over the place."

"No," said Salvatore, "it was fine with us. They were very generous. The Germans collected every drop of material, every crumb. If they saw a civilian looking at an empty can, they shot him. But the Americans, *mamma mia . . .*"

Sweet Pietro had only been six at the time. But even he remembered: cans half full of oil, cans of gas, discarded jackets, biscuits, chocolates, ammunition cases, webbed belts, boots, single gloves, canteens, cardboard boxes. Once an American soldier came over especially to give him a can with chocolate in it, then came running back a minute later to give him biscuits and a kiss.

"Oh Pietro," Sarah said, "did you have big round eyes and a dirty face and curls?"

He showed them a snapshot, with clean face, but round eyes, curls, and a white suit with short pants.

"So much stuff," Salvatore said, gruffly. "People made a living on it. So many machines, so much fire power. The Germans said we were afraid to fight the Americans, but the Americans were worse soldiers than ours. They just had all the machines."

"But did people want to resist?" Howard asked. "Did they want to fight for the Germans?"

"The Germans were lower than beasts. That's not the point. I'm just saying — for bravery, match a Sicilian against an American any time. See what happens."

Howard looked down, as if something had nipped at his ankles. "That's a pretty strange thing to worry about. In any case, Americans don't like to be soldiers. Luckily for the world."

"Why, luckily?"

In a hurry, Pietro said, "Somebody told me about a new pizza restaurant in Catania that has a big face of Polifemo with his mouth wide open. That's where they shove the pies. It's a kind of oven."

"Pietro, don't tell us you've never been to Catania!" said Sarah.

"I've never been anywhere. Just twice to Palermo."

The rain stopped and they left Empedocle, grinding up the hill, crossing the wind-driven orchards and fields toward Agrigento again.

Sarah asked whether the great Pirandello's house wasn't supposed to be somewhere near Agrigento. Pietro was thrilled that all the world knew Pirandello, who wrote tales in *their* dialect about their lives. Salvatore called him *stupido* and said that people in Europe and America only read some plays that he had written in Italian. The younger boy looked to Howard as impartial expert, who said, true, he only knew of *Six Characters in Search of an Author,* (Which, however, he had not read. Sarah had, in high school, and again in a course called "Drama of Today." Howard wasn't much on literature after Virgil.) They pulled up at a stone cottage on the edge of a wasted field. Pirandello's house.

Starting with writers, the talk swiftly turned to bombing. Salvatore had been in the fields near here when the American planes roared over, blowing up trees, sheep, everything. Who knows how they missed Pirandello's cottage? A miracle.

"Why," asked Howard (ignoring Sarah's squeeze of caution), "should they have wanted to hit his cottage? You talk as if they came here because they wanted to destroy."

"No. They came here as good people. Simple people. Maybe that's why they didn't know how to make war. Look, if the Germans start bombing sheep, it's because they decide on that as good tactics, or they prefer to make things die. The British always pinpoint military targets. The British and the Germans, they are experts at making war. They hit what they want. But the Americans — boom, boom, boom — hit a house, hit a gun, hit a farm, kill a family, then *ecco!*" Salvatore began to play "Anchors Aweigh" on a mock trombone, sliding his tough hand back and forth, daa-da-da-DA-di-DA . . . "*I liberatori!* Chocolates! Caramels! Wave the hand!" Abruptly, he stopped.

"It must have been miserable," Howard said, slowly. "But we didn't ask to come here. We didn't start the war. However, we sure finished it."

"That you did."

"War, war, war," said Pietro. "Turridu. Owda. The hell with the war, eh? It's been over for fifteen years."

"Yes," Sarah said. "Let's talk about something important."

"Like how we shall arrange for the Festival, and for the party with Salvatore's uncle," added Pietro.

Salvatore drove off in a sudden swerve and a moment later screeched to a stop that jumbled the contents of his car. "Everybody out!" he shouted.

It was the edge of a flourishing orchard. He leaped out ahead, grasped an almond branch in each hand, snapped them off with quick strong wrists. "A humble offering for two noble visitors!"

The red-hearted, white blossoms were floppier, more ample than Sarah had thought. She buried her face in them and the sweet spring raindrops came off upon her cheeks and forehead.

Howard rubbed the soaked black bark, exchanged smiles with Salvatore, gave a speech of thanks.

All four stood, touched.

The sky was still a scudding gray, but Pietro promised that tomorrow would be splendid. He pointed out pale gaps and made the Americans turn to see a long stripe of orange against the sea at the west.

"But Salvatore," said Sarah, "you didn't have to break off so much for us. Just look at all these dead almonds."

"*Beh,* my family used to own this orchard. Mama received a Mussolini Harvest Prize once." This was some kind of joke between the boys and further eased the mood. He turned to Howard. "Have you ever tasted real *torrone?* . . . No, no, not that glue they sell in stores in Rome. My mama makes it out of nothing but almonds and honey. I'll have her make a batch for you and Sara before the Festival."

"Please now, don't trouble —"

But Salvatore said it was a great delicacy and they would be imbeciles to have been here without tasting it. Also they should not forget that they would all be together at the party tomorrow night at the uncle's — they remembered the fat man who drives busses?

Pietro was nodding, yes, yes, his eyes soft at the prospect of being among old and new friends.

Howard said, "Then, would you let us do just one thing? Take you out with us to dinner tonight?"

No, they had already planned to have "some fish" with Salvatore's mama. And they thought the Americans would like to be alone for a while to talk and . . . you know. Also tomorrow, Salvatore said, if there was a desire to look at the museum or at stones, they would not disturb.

"I know what you'll let us do," Sarah said, admonishing the boys with mock-serious eyebrows and index finger. "Tomorrow will be beautiful and you will come to a picnic with us. That's an order."

Excellent. Americans to provide meat, cheese, whatever they want; Sicilians to bring wine and coffee. But where?

Howard wanted to look closely at the huge ruins of Olympian Zeus, where one of the telamones, the giant stone men, still lay as he had fallen.

"Of course," said Pietro. "*Il gigante!* Let's have the picnic at *il gigante!*"

"On *il gigante!*" Salvatore corrected.

In town, among increasing crowds, they parted warmly, until early next afternoon on the giant.

That night the room seemed still tighter, the walls thinner. Raucousness an inch outside their door broke a moment when the tall husband and wife might have moved together. Howard sat on the edge of the bed, chin in hand,

and Sarah, although she wanted to protest against his sacrificing himself for her sleep, was too tired to form the words.

6

"NOT a cloud south of Naples," the radio in the coffee
bar had bragged; now, after hours among the sun-
warmed antiquities, the Americans were laying out their
picnic on oiled paper: marinated artichoke hearts, olives
they had chosen from thick barrels of brine, Genoa salami,
crude prosciutto in streaks of dark red, provolone cheese,
plum tomatoes, goat's cheese, glossy pimentos, oranges,
and loaves of bread. Bright lizards stuck out their tongues
and flashed back into hiding between the stone discs of the
giant's body. Since their lunch made glistenings and
blotches where time had flattened the telamon's stomach,
Howard felt entitled to explain how this twenty-five-foot
stone man came to be lying in sunbath position, elbows
folded back alongside his face: how the Greek colonists
won an amazing battle over the Carthaginians — on the
same day as Salamis, they say — which brought Akragas all
her wealth and power, and this temple of Olympian Zeus
was to be the first built in celebration. But it was mon-
strous, Oriental, Hollywoodian in dimension, with these
stone *gigante*'s to add support between the colossal columns,
and it fell in of its own weight, having killed God knows
how many slaves and overseers first and leaving our quiet
stone friend here, as he lies. Howard forgot that he had
told the same story yesterday. Sarah stroked the erosions
on the vast stone face; a few thousand years of wind and

rain had worn away all features except his eye caverns. She was saying, "Poor man, doesn't the sun make you giddy?" as the two boys came up through the grass, each holding one handle of a heavy suitcase.

It contained: a clean white tablecloth, chinaware plates, four red and white napkins, silver fork-knife-and-spoon for each, stemmed wine glasses, three bottles of wine, a bowl of sugar, coffee cups with saucers, a gleaming pot full of hot espresso, small spoons, and a cardboard box that had "some sweets."

Both boys wore short-sleeved sport shirts: Salvatore's motley, Pietro's demure. Pietro kicked at a lizard. "Now if *il gigante* will just keep the coffee warm." He rested the pot on the giant's hot flat sternum. Sun silver flared along the stone.

"I thought this was supposed to be *our* picnic," Howard said.

"It is, it is," said Salvatore. "We've only brought the extras."

The Americans, both wearing soft-collared tennis shirts, both showing healthy chests to the sun, watched a formal table being set along *il gigante*'s abdomen.

Pietro settled cross-legged upon the ground, pleased to be looking up. Salvatore and Sarah each chose a thigh, and Howard, uneasy at first, arranged his buttocks in the telamon's eye caverns.

That picnic was to Illinois picnics as Carnival to Lent. It was decided that with the olives, artichokes, and salami, the local red wine would go best; with the prosciutto and cheese courses, the cool white Soave from Verona; and to carry on to the end, the Marsala from eastern Sicily, syrupy, redolent of almonds. At first — decorum;

red and white napkins tucked into collars. Then inevitably oil got onto fingers, vinegar onto cheeks, wines on upper lips and tablecloth. Afternoon heat softened the meats and cheeses, made hands langorous and inaccurate in the passing of food, smoothed the pouring of wine into stem glass and throat. Laughter began, grew hilarious because life presented itself as absurd and memorable. Cypresses, evergreens, almonds and olives; unblemished sky and time-tempered architecture; still grasses, poppies, quick orange lizards and yellow birds; the pleasure of blond hair and dark muscular forearms; the fallen temple and all fallen things no matter how venerable on which today they put their bottoms to eat and drink, and the passing tide of visitors who never dared suggest that such contemporary riot be evicted from the hallowed place; so many things to toast (birthdays, Pirandello, the new Pope), and always the sea, spread wide and dazzling beyond them.

"What will *gigante* think of all this?" asked Howard.

"He has had enough time to think," Salvatore said.

Pietro talked for the first time of his father, a master cart maker. Once he had told a tourist how to look for the name of the carver on the back end of the design, and as the tourist — a tall Englishman — stooped over to follow close behind a cart, the donkey suddenly stopped but the Englishman didn't, so he walked face first into the back-board and lost two teeth.

They drank to him.

"Ah, tourists, tourists," Salvatore said. His knife glinted in the sun again as he cut the scarlet-and-opium-and-lime-colored sweets. "But never have we had a time like this with tourists. There is something different about you, something human. You understand so much."

Pietro bubbled, "Listen to Turridu! Trying to flatter. Last night at dinner I was complimenting your Italian to him. He said, 'Yes, with them at least the words can be distinguished one from another.' "

Sarah threw an olive at Salvatore, saying, "Oh, you beast!" The sturdy pale-eyed man told her to throw another, which he caught in his mouth, applauding himself.

Howard told about an old lady in Palermo who grew furious with him because he didn't recognize a picture of her nephew, a barber in Los Angeles.

Pietro said, "Hi, baby," in English to everybody who passed by, to male German tour guides, to two silvery British matrons.

Sarah, stroking a stone drum of the giant's thigh and looking at the sky, said something about a bird which turned out to be an inconceivably dirty word in Italian, causing hysteria and blushes and doublings-up and waving of red napkins under the sunlight.

Howard did a handstand. The Sicilians performed a leapfrog. They had a cavalry battle, Pietro and Sarah as knights, Salvatore and Howard as bulky steeds.

After the oranges and coffee and last drops of sweet dark Marsala, Howard stretched out full length on the ground, parallel to the giant, saying, "Ohmigod, ohmigod." Pietro was moved again at all the confluence of accidents that had to happen for them to have these hours together; Sarah, humming a tune, was thinking of living in the sun forever; Salvatore was placing his beret where *gigante*'s nose had once been, as a pillow, when Howard, all wine-muddled and sun-coaxed, had a Reflection. Instantaneously, everything seemed clear: they had come away so far to measure the deeds of dead Greek men but had found instead something alive, something living — a live god of Sicily. Who? Where? Bright sky and landscape blurred, for they had been sitting on him, setting great red and green bottles upon him! It was Telamon-Cyclops, Gigante-Polifemo, the toppler and the toppled one, piler of big stones and knocker-down of temples, one-eyed Lord of the Carnival oozing lizards and jeered by little dark men, lounger in the sun with missing face and body of thunderous stone discs . . . Howard slept; he was very drunk.

When they awakened him the sun was far down and all the bottles, trash, utensils had been packed away in the car. Talk was subdued. As he bent to tie a shoelace, his head gave a harsh throb. Lips and cheeks burned from the sun-sleep.

Then they were in the car, Howard cramped into fetal position, leaving town, temple, tourists behind, and jostling down toward a promenade by the sea. It was a good day for San Leone. They passed bent men, chopping at the fields. Patient donkeys nodded.

"Wine makes dreams," Salvatore said.

"I dreamed of the *gigante*," said Howard, "but I can't remember what. Things happened, stones fell. Someone kept saying, 'Polifemo did it.' "

Salvatore interpreted that as Pietro, because it was the wretched boy's only explanation for things.

Sarah said, "Oh, I wish I could remember dreams. Last night I had a terrible one. In the morning I forgot everything, except that it was fascinating."

"You dreamed of the black grape," said Pietro, laughing to her.

"Is that good or bad?"

"Oh, it's nothing. It's something my mother used to say

about her dreams. When she did, you could always tell she was going to make confession that day."

At San Leone, the summer villas and ice cream shops were shuttered, leaving the beach and sea clean for rare strollers. Wind had begun, with a smell of late warmth. The sun rolled low, but its blaze still atomized in the white crash of breakers, then formed again, coalesced upon the retreat of the water, and again shattered and flashed into a chaos of light, and again coalesced into calm brilliant displays. The four stood, quiet, backs to the green land.

Watery crashings, siftings, wind brought memories.

Pietro said they used to play here, after the war had passed, every day.

"Here is where the Americans landed," said Salvatore.

He described it, the relief when the crisis, the firings, the corpses finally began. His descriptions were solid, like himself, palpable.

Sarah's closed eyes were to the sun, the wind, the mild spray. She was tired of words.

But the waves and words had excited Howard into reflections again. If he was dizzy, still he was awake this time, had not seen the sea often in his life, and couldn't resist whispering into Sarah's ear how ironic it was, how fantastic to be standing here now, hearing only about the Americans' landing of a few years ago, when on this same beach, on days like this, Phoenician traders had rolled up their boats, the colonists from Rhodes had landed, and Carthaginian invaders, Romans, Arabs, Spaniards . . . All those sails, those men . . .

While he was whispering into Sarah's right ear, Salvatore, to her left, light with wine, was pressing his thick bare arm against hers (warm, and softly downed), watching intently for a reaction. He then stroked faintly once or twice the sensitive hollow where her arm creased. Wine, sun, sea, wind, whisperings from stirred husband, fingertips of stirred and generous host: Sarah's sensations lacked order.

Pietro, from the far end of the row, observed all, cursing a number of gods at once.

Surprising, the care it can take just to ease a long-legged girl into a miniature Italian car. Howard was still dazed at history's sails riding off the shore, so it was up to Salvatore to guide and squeeze her arm, his work-darkened nails faintly blanching with the pressure. He had to make sure that she sat comfortably in the inadequate space, that her skirt was not in danger from the door.

"Let's go, Owda," Pietro called. "It's getting late."

The blond man settled in, making the car rock on its springs.

They rode back past wind-ravaged olive trees, through a world tossing with long orange light. Sarah allowed herself an image she would have ridiculed from anyone else: the rough olive trees as masculine, the puffs of almond, of course, feminine. Passing the ridge of temples, they saw that it was becoming a fairgrounds of visitors, motorcycles, bright preparations for the folk dancing tomorrow.

Salvatore talked about the exercises he did every morning, the lifting of weights. His mama and sisters laughed at him for it, but the body should be kept strong. He swerved often, and leaned on the horn.

Pietro told Howard and Sarah that if they would only take him out of Sicily in their suitcase, he would build them better temples than these.

Howard said this was the best day they had had in Europe.

Sarah blinked at them all, wondering whether to be amused or in a mild panic.

7

Oн this early evening, *passeggiata* was a turmoil. Agrigento's twisting street had become a funnel through which bodies poured — every man and boy from miles of southern Sicily — until the town filled to its brim. Packed, they strolled from one end to the other, and down again. There was a carelessness about the jostling of bodies. There was little attempt to conceal the point of remarks about tourists bent over their tables in the restaurants or still buying cork models of the temples in shops. Girls watched from third-floor windows. Twilight slid over rooftops and down alleys to mingle with the splashed electric light. In the turmoil, there was latent tomorrow's greater turmoil: Festival. Snatches of color and the old music flew in from squares to the side, where floats were being touched up; the new music blared from coffee bars; spirits were rising.

But not Pietro's. Arm in arm with Salvatore, he had just suggested that they not see the Americans any more.

"What do you mean?" his friend snapped. He was almost angry. "Tomorrow we show them the Festival. Tonight they're coming to Uncle's party." Leave it to Pietro to cast gloom over the one interesting day of the year.

"You are a dog, Turridu. After we all pledge friendship, you start stroking Sara every time he turns his back."

"It's not my fault. You know I'd rather have honest friendship than to steal a woman for an hour."

This was Pietro's chance to pull his eye open to the glistening red.

Salvatore said, "But she is expressing herself with her legs. Whether she knows it or not. Say she doesn't, but it makes me nervous."

"The television says in America they have tranquil pills. Better ask Owda for one."

"For two days you can trust me. We give them a good time for the Festival and the next day they're gone. Don't worry."

Salvatore exchanged brilliant insults with a passing friend. He was much respected as a man, even though he worked so hard. Pietro softened to his usual consistency and drifted into what Salvatore called, "one of your recitations." It was a fantasy in which Salvatore has a baby by Sarah. The baby is of course an American citizen and its first words will be to request that its papa, Salvaturi Turridu Castagnolo, be admitted to America on the preferred list as immediate family. Thus, having been typically calculating, he will go, make millions, be happy. And Pietro, the little friend? Having been typically sweet and letting his female guests alone, he will be in this abandoned hole until the day he dies, looking for Fiats or donkeys to repair . . .

The street was thinning. Pietro said if they were under twelve they could go to the movies free. James Dean was playing. He still thought that would be better than the Carnival party.

Salvatore asked, with some concern, "Do you want to be a child all your life?"

"Yes."

"Why? Don't be an imbecile."

"Less trouble. More sweets."

Salvatore hit him over the head with his floppy beret, laughed.

They went up the hill in the Topolino to fetch the Americans.

8

Uncle-bus-driver, cheeks round and pink from a fresh shave, was desolate at not having seen Howard and Sarah for two days. However, he said they would all make up for it tonight and he offered them, at the door, two glasses of a heavy licorice liqueur. Sarah said, no, kind man, perhaps later; they had drunk so much sweet wine that afternoon.

(She had fallen asleep as soon as the boys had dropped them at their room, while Howard sat on the edge of the bed beginning to enter reflections into his journal. She was going to mention Salvatore's latest tricks of hospitality, but then, *why bother*? A moment's flirtation was the least she could give in return for all that local-color generosity. At least it would make a punctuation mark for her in the lines that Howard's right hand was already laying out, like a reaper with his crops. Or was it a sower? She never could keep these agricultural similes straight . . . It seemed the next minute that the Topolino horn had awakened them both, bleating from the street below, which was full of night. They had had no supper.)

But Uncle said he refused to be punished just because Salvatore, that notorious rapscallion, had already filled them full of Marsala. It was Festival, it was Carnival, and he wanted all his guests to be happy. They drank.

It was a narrow, poor house in the center of the town,

crammed tonight with little girls jumping up and down in lavender dresses, with older girl cousins, men who wore their black best and shook hands with passion, Uncle's wife and mother and her sisters; also Salvatore's mama, who was ample, quiet, and almost toothless, who embraced both Americans because her son hadn't been so interested by meeting people in years and if they impressed *him* they must be wonderful people.

Francesca was presented — a girl with shrewd eyes and radiant black hair.

Said Uncle in a stage whisper: "We hope to settle Salvatore down, and this is our bait. What do you think?"

Francesca shook hands with self-assured courtesy. She said, "The Uncle exaggerates."

Uncle's father, whose fingers were gnarled as old potatoes, tottered about pouring tumblers of red wine for everyone, and the music was turned on. The bare center of the floor was for dancing, the straight chairs along the wall for resting. The music was the coffee-bar music, the jukebox music, on records. At one end of the room the Virgin ascended in glazed stucco relief with two technicolor assistants in flowing robes. There Pietro stood, alien and haughty in pressed black, pretending to study the composition. All the others, except the aged or tiny, danced, quite decorously. The air was close, hot, inevitably grew closer, hotter. The floor had room only for careful milling, particularly when Howard and Sarah danced, looming like pneumatic prodigies and growing self-conscious, beginning to sweat profusely in the sweaters they had put over their soft tennis shirts. Salvatore and Francesca, dancing close to them, tried to put them at their ease with a conspiracy against Pietro. Howard was sent off to request a dance from one of the cousins, a charming chipmunk of a girl whose face turned scarlet as he ambled up to her and who managed only by judicious stretching to get her free arm around him and above his belt line. They conversed in textbook phrases about the preferability of holidays to ordinary days, while "You Are My Destiny" boomed from the record player, she trying to hide her terrror that he might with a surprise step squelch her from this world; and all her friends and relatives giggled behind their hands.

This left Sarah, willowy and alone. Salvatore and Francesca with a posse of eight-year-olds marched on Pietro to press him into service as her dance partner. A joyous scuffle was anticipated. But he ruined the scene by being perfectly willing; he shook off his tormentors and approached Sarah with archaic courtesy. They danced, he from a distance, seeming not so much shorter as off to the side and beneath her, like one of the attendants of the Ascending Virgin.

Most picturesque and Festive, the mixing of human hues and sizes now. Uncle beamed. "You Are My Destiny" perfidiously began to play again without having stopped, and the chipmunk girl threw a look past Howard's chest at the culprits. The hot room brought color into the faces of both Americans as they looked down at their partners, but gone was the threat of blushes. Each wore a fine blond wine flush.

For a moment while the rest of the room looked cheery or beatific, Salvatore glowered. He glowered at Pietro and Sarah in their stately dance; from the corners of her eyes Francesca watched him.

There was applause when the music stopped. The girl cousin skittered away from Howard toward her friends, and Salvatore came up, jarringly demonstrative. "Owda, Sara, superb! You look superb among us!"

They thanked him.

"But we don't have the *torrone* for you yet," he said. "I don't know how to apologize. Mama wants it to be just right, just pure and sweet. I hope, I *promise* for tomorrow!"

Again they thanked him; they certainly didn't want it to be cause for worry.

Francesca had taken a stand next to him. "Turridu is afraid you will miss some of the touristic pleasures while you are here. He would take the blame on himself."

She appraised Howard. He took in her strong face, the sense of her womanliness, her poise. A pinpoint of interest grew keen within him. Wine, heat, the confusions of these days — much of course could have encouraged it.

The room was circling to a new record. Francesca, as she danced with Howard, gave him a light pound on the back, and said, "You are terrifying."

"Why?"

"That little girl — the cousin — whom you danced with, said, 'He's like a mountain. What if he falls on me?' "

"I don't fall on people."

Howard had a vestige of daylight sense which insisted that this was a devious girl. He wasn't sure why. But he *was* sure that he could be trusted as a gentleman, would always be one.

"You are bored with us," Francesca said.

"On the contrary. Much too much on the contrary."

"Ah, we are taking too much of your time. You wanted to see antiquity. You would prefer us to be doing the tarantella tonight. In old costumes."

(In fact, Howard had entered these lines into his journal: *I have not availed myself of the unique opportunities of-*

fered here to observe the archaeological superimpositions of distinctive civilizations one upon the other, leaving unique continuities, nor have I found the time to absorb unhampered the tranquility and power of the Doric temples. I hope that an acquaintance with the local mores will compensate in part. Tonight we go to a Carnival party, escorted by our two adhesive (but kindly) cicerones, where perhaps a glimpse of tarantellas and such holdovers from the pre-industrial past will prevent the time from being completely wasted.)

"Do you know everybody's secrets?" he asked.

"There are no secrets." She began not to laugh when she said this; but then she did.

Sarah and Salvatore were dancing in complete silence. She was sure their silence would be overheard. He was taking advantage of her hips' swerving higher than his, to make constant minor adjustments with his arm. The only words he had spoken had to do with the top of her khaki skirt — it was slippery, he said. She didn't understand the adjective. Therefore he dramatized its meaning with his hands, slipping here and there. He looked either away or right into the center of her eyes, like a movie lover. The whole thing was really getting out of hand; it was not quite laughable.

"Salvatore —" she began.

"No need to speak," said he, and fixed her again with pale eyes.

The dance was over and dark Pietro was standing among them, apparently to keep the same alignments from occurring again. Francesca was amused at everything that Pietro did. She called him "the little spoon" because he was always stirring up a new *minestra*. The tempo was quickening. It was getting harder to hear voices well. Wine circulated. A deputation of tiny girls tugged at Sarah's skirt, then blushed and stuttered at their own boldness. She bent over and three of them whispered an impassioned spate into her ear. She nodded her head (causing ecstasy and flight), straightened up and punched Howard in the arm, good-fellow style.

"Well, Owda old man, we have a request from the public to do *une exhibition* in the center ring. I hope you're in good shape."

He looked at her, startled. Salvatore said that one should never exchange private remarks in a foreign language among company that doesn't understand it; after all, none of them were using Sicilian dialect.

Sarah gave him a quizzical look. Francesca said, "Turridu is such a strict one, about other people's manners."

Sarah said, in Italian, "They want us to dance a rock-and-roll. Can one refuse?"

Pietro snorted. "How crude!" He sent a threatening glance to the high-keyed knot of girls, one of whom stuck her tongue out at him.

"Oh, poor Americans," Francesca said. "They have come far, far to see the tarantella and now instead they have to show their native dances." Howard frowned, somewhere near the ceiling.

A bargain was made: A tarantella for a rock-and-roll. Straight exchange basis. The news traveled through the party, finding almost every young man, Pietro and Salvatore included, more than ready to throw off his jacket for an old-fashioned whirl, now that it was rescued by official sanction from seeming too rustic. They crowded around and the room became unified. Uncle could not be found, but they were sure he wouldn't mind. The girls took off their high-heeled shoes.

But the record collection included no tarantellas. Never mind, they all knew a tune, and the room suddenly filled with amateur music produced on that orchestral clown, the body. Some whistled, some puffed their cheeks for the bullfrog oompa-oompa, some hummed, some sang fa-la-la, bystanders stamped feet and clapped hands, Uncle's father knew how to sound like a fiddle. Pietro turned out to be nimble, a hop-hop-hopper; Salvatore, surprisingly easy on his feet for a blocky man; Francesca, efficient. The sounds, the swirls, quick beat, happy unembarrassed faces flying in passage made a wondrous tarantella for Howard and Sarah to see, standing arm in arm to the side, pleased and touched, stamping to time.

There was great heat in the room. The dancers, reveling in tiredness, gulped at wine. The old assured the Americans, that's the way parties used to be; and Francesca, with a streak of hair wet across her temples, her whole face in a better temper, congratulated Howard as if he had thought up a new party game.

No trouble to find a rock-and-roll record in the collection — there were eleven — but the question was, which? It was eagerly put to the Americans. They were swept into the general absurdity, not resisting. Above the babble rose Howard's voice, deciding for "Rock, Rock, Around the Clock," a sentimental choice "to commemorate the first evening of friendship with Pietro and Turridu," who stood happily nodding and drenched in perspiration.

"*One* o'clock, *two* o'clock, *three* o'clock *ROCK* . . ."

The floor hadn't shaken under the tarantella, but it did under Howard's colossal legs and Sarah's body when he allowed her to come to ground between hurtlings. Along the four walls the hands beat to time, smiles were pasted. The old looked on in fascination and fright, but the young

were at a circus. This was what they wanted — transatlantic
frenzy, embodied movies. It wasn't expert rock-and-roll —
Howard and Sarah were a generation too late for that —
but wild it was, and on the beat, and acrobatic. Howard
had gone into a gust of joy just to be *doing* something,
leaping, moving, tossing another body, not standing, not
cramped. Sarah's hair flew. Her arms shone. He handled
her like a matchstick, threw her out, pulled her back,
flicked her over his hip. She cried out once as she sailed by,
"Hey you wanna break my ass?" The audience cheered,
missing her words, but not the meaning. Again, the record
replayed without a break. Their bodies fell into the oblivi-
ous swerve and jolt of rhythm. The faces at the walls faded.
Eyes were nothing, beat was all. The two were out of themselves now, two blond kids dancing in Illinois, dancing
better than they ever had before, far better, on a downstate
Saturday night while for a thousand miles to left and right
blond kids were dancing, a wide night with its whole
generation rocking around the clock, out, back, up and
past, out, back around the back, out, back, back to back . . .

Salvoes of applause. The music was over. Faces returned,
admiring; the little girls were in a drastic state of over-
stimulation. Older girls looked up at Howard, who was
panting, glowing, standing with arms loose; their eyes
struggled with impermissible thoughts. The clusterers
around Sarah had given in: honey is honey. To each other
the two sent a quick look, and it was eloquent. Never before had they danced into such wildness, not even in college. Why not? Why out of nowhere tonight?

Talk poured around them, all the questions about
America that had courteously been held in check now
flowed over the sluiceways opened by music. Tell us about
the space, the money, the cars, the movement, the crime,

the Negroes, New York. What do you think about all the
Sicilian gangsters? Are you afraid of the Russians? Is all the
food frozen? Do you live as in the movies? Does anyone
there read Dante or Manzoni? Do you know so-and-so in
Chicago, in San Francisco, in McKeesport, Pennsylvania?

Pietro proudly stood guard, helping them find words,
rejecting the unanswerable questions. When the two
seemed hesitant, or tired of answering, he improvised fill-
ins, such as: "In America the milk is good. That's because
the grass is sweet, the cows are healthy and tranquil.
People grow up tall. Here the milk is bitter, because the
grass is sour. Our grass isn't even green. The cows just look
at it and they lose their appetites." The surrounders would
laugh at him, some affectionately, some not, and he would
say, "Owda. Sara. Isn't that so? *You* tell them," and
Salvatore would play the caustic commentator on his
friend's notions, saying, "Eh, Pietro, maybe we should make
our cows wear green spectacles, eh? Maybe that would
help." When the talk quieted a bit, turning to gentle questions about their families, it seemed to the Americans that
the party was ending and that they had provided its real
center. They were not displeased.

However, they were wrong. Through the far door an
apparition entered the room at full speed, squealing — a
fat, fat woman whose breasts bounced from shoulders to
waistline as she ran and whose mouth, lipsticked from ear
to ear, howled for help. The fat woman was Uncle, wearing
a straw wig and rouge and an orange blouse with grapefruits bouncing inside of it, and a motley peasant skirt
and then hairy legs with bus driver's shoes. She screamed
again and all the children fled to the walls. But not from
Uncle. Another had bounded into the room in hot pursuit
of her. His face was streaked with charcoal and he had a

charcoal mustache drawn askew to make his mouth a
caricature of drunkenness, and his black vest flapped open
over bare stomach, and his peasant knickers had the fly
open, and hanging from his fly was a long limp sausage.
Uncle raised her fat arms and flew a circle around the room
while *he* staggered after, leering and working his char-
coaled chops, his sausage flopping. The room was a din.
He caught her, kissed her squealing face, squeezed the
grapefruits. She slapped his hand. He reached into her
blouse, took out one of the grapefruits, which turned out
to be an orange — a huge Sicilian globe of an orange — and
ran around the room in triumph, holding it aloft and
squeezing it with both hands, while Uncle waddled in pursuit, crying, "Give it back! Give it back!" Uncle caught
him because he had stopped to slurp at someone's wine.
She got the orange away from him and back into her blouse,
slapped his face, with a most realistic crack. He turned
furious, lunged for her rear parts and missed, sprawling
on the floor. Uncle jumped up and down and chittered.
The pursuer got up, brushed off his vest and sausage, and
then began the serious chase. He only failed to catch her
because he stopped to drink from everyone's wine glass
(except the Americans'), and stopped in front of the little
girls to shake his sausage at them while they died in mock
terror and hid their faces. His face was a smear of charcoal and red wine. He did catch her. They began to dance,
to a record that had begun to play on cue, full volume.
Their dance was a parody of ballroom customs, with much
bowing and curtseying and both their mouths going at
once, spewing double-talk. They swept the room in an
egregious waltz, bumping into everyone, knocking glasses
over, until he suddenly reached in for her breasts again,
extracted one (while she beamed and implanted lipstick on

his cheek), peeled it, and began to eat. Beaming, she pulled out his sausage, which was attached by a string to his belt, cut the string, and also began to eat. They smacked their lips, eyed each other in adoration. The room went helpless with gasped laughter, demure screams, accusations of *terrible!* The two players bowed and exited, to a wreckage of applause and hoots.

Pietro's eyes were burning. "I am mortified. Mortified!" he said, to Howard and Sarah. "I had no idea they were planning to do the skit. I beg you to believe me! I never would have allowed that you come. You see how we are here — animals. Beasts!" He turned on Salvatore. "You didn't tell me your Uncle was going to do it! You weren't honest." He turned back to Sarah, rubbing his hands in dismay, "Please believe me, signora Sara!"

(She was seeing everything in a displacement, saw Pietro as saying, "Oh, my dear paws! Oh, my fur and whiskers! What *will* the duchess think?" Or again, as a Victorian figure, announcing to his lifelong friend, "Sir, you are not a gentleman!") For the moment, she could find nothing to say. She nodded vaguely, recognized that Francesca wanted to exchange patronizing looks with her, over Pietro, but she refused.

"When else should they do it?" said Salvatore, airily. "Owda and Sara want to see the world. This is how our Carnival is. They wouldn't want us to change it, just for them." He put his arm around his friend, who shook it off, and he looked with a question toward his guests.

"Of course not," Howard said. He gave Pietro's shoulder a friendly shake. "Of course we wouldn't. You don't have to protect us, Pietro."

Sarah agreed. But she hoped she was controlling her color. (Look who's becoming a prude! That mad Dashner

girl, she told herself, turning into Shocked Sorority Sister
number one.)

Howard and Salvatore laughed and drank by themselves
for a moment, in a corner. They were enchanging lists
of filthy words from their languages, Howard itching to
record them in his journal before he forgot. Salvatore had
begun to remind him of a certain kind of athlete — built
close to the ground, hard to budge, sure of himself to the
edge of arrogance.

Sarah and Francesca alternated with Pietro, one comforting and the other ridiculing.

Now all the guests came past Howard and Sarah to bid
their good-nights, wishes for pleasant sleep, gratitude for
the dancing and the conversation, wishes for happy Festival.

The last little lavender girls had been herded out, still
tittering, and the ancient had gone with brittle steps. The
wreckage of the room swam into focus, the spilled glasses,
the old poor walls, the chairs at crazy angles, and through
it came Uncle, neatly dressed but his mouth still blurred,
and with him his pursuer, who now clearly was the artist
who had been on the ladder two nights ago painting
Polifemo; he still wore the same gray business suit.

Uncle extended soft hands to Howard and Sarah. He
said he was so content that they could come to his little
evening; he hoped they hadn't been too offended by the
little Carnival joke. Not in the least, they said. They
thanked him warmly for his hospitality. He said the pleasure had been all his own, and began pouring liqueur for
them. But really they thought it was time to leave the
family some holiday privacy. Protests, back and forth.
Salvatore finally insisted that he drive them home at least.
Howard almost too abruptly said, no, no! They could use
a ten-minute stroll through the air.

Plans were left vague for tomorrow's Festival, Howard saying he wanted to see a few things in the morning while Sarah rested. But they could meet toward noon for a *passeggiata* before the parade of floats began. Sarah saved her last good-night, her richest smile for Pietro, who almost stopped rubbing his paws and whiskers.

Then again they were out beneath the Mediterranean night, which bathed the shuttered town in fragrance and star shadows, with hushings from beyond the hilltop that might have come from the sea, might have come from trees. They breathed.

"Well," said Sarah. "That was quite a party."

9

As they went up the dark twisting street Howard lectured about their luck in having witnessed a survival of ancient spring rites, pagan, even Dionysian, you might say, and he dilated on his theme as if arguing before a review board of professors who had not taken him seriously enough when he was a football player. So often he argued before that board when he could have been talking to her. His arm was around her in the groove it had worn, but his head drifted on above, impersonal, pale, voluble, and by the time they climbed their back staircase set out against the heave of massed and night-illumined hills, Sarah was tense.

For hundreds of nights, how many hundred nights, on another continent, Howard's body had rioted over hers! Even early, when her wit was still set against him, her spread body had allowed him anything. Later, much had become routine. He grew distracted more and more often; strangely abstract. Still they had great gifts — health, lust, beauty — which they had not feared to enjoy. There had been sickness outside in the American night, but it could not touch them. Yet again, they had loved always in quiet rooms, big rooms, big beds, surrounded by thick walls and floor and ceiling, with shower room nearby and stacked with clean towels, even the field of play covered with fresh sheets, perhaps midnight music on the radio. He wanted it that way, and so that was the way it had been. He loved silently; she had taught her tongue not to play. Now the rusty wash of light from the olive-bulb threw shadows across their faces. Shadows of hunger. They were jammed against each other in that tight room, and jammed against their room was another from which the old music of bedsprings was playing again, crescendo, to a libretto of giggles, moans, nipping noises, jokes: even the words could be distinguished one from another.

No words in their own room, but two naked bodies, long, aroused, uneasy. He had to feel alone with her. If not, then a crowd might as well have been leering. And although hungry, he would freeze. Into their silence came buttings from the other side of the wall, with stronger groans. His need for silence was what she blamed; she saw no need for it. And more than silence, he always needed: abstraction. But for once she wanted to be exactly who and where she was. On impulse, she decided to caper, to change a seven-year mood. ("When in Rome . . .") Play, and laughter: "Dig that crazy sausage!" Her laugh was hopeful, a rumor of more antic lives; but he pulled back to his pillow.

She refused to look punished.

"I guess this isn't the time," he said, quietly, without hostility.

But that was the only time they could have seized, in Agrigento.

After a while, the next room slackened into peace. Moonlight arrived and began to travel the floor. Sarah couldn't sleep. She was tense with need, tense with the absolute conviction that he missed the point in everything. He wouldn't take time to devise new love, he wouldn't even take time for new talk. New life came, and he directed

himself forthwith to record it into some vast pattern that
could exist only in the dome of his head. He allowed no
messy personal seepage. They had seen new life here; it
had shaken both of them, strangely. She was sure of that.
But he would never let himself admit being shaken, would
never allow seepage of something strange. Then he was in
for trouble, and she was sure of that, too. Things seep
down, whether you admit it or not, my righteous husband,
my upstanding model of outmoded disciplines, my model-T
Greek. He tossed, with his eyes closed but his pale lips
working. See? There they go, seeping. Things always do.
You sleep, they seep. *Mens sana, in corpore* Sani-Flush. He
tossed again, hair falling across his serious forehead. She
wanted to knock there again, to laugh at somebody who
lived there, to show him in her own way how highly she
still held him for trying so hard when all the rest of the
world said, *Why bother?* To help him, by the laughter he
needed, by being easy. Lovers were two halves of one, op-
posites that join. She kissed his forehead and his cheek
and his temple, knowing that if she woke him in just the
right way now, then everything could be done easily and
well in the quiet traveling moonlight. It had worked before. But he tossed violently, turned his back to her. She
went tense, strange, in part because her quick memory
played a trick, delving up lines she had hardly heard since
her days of "There will be time to murder and create":

> *She shall not kiss that harried one*
> *To peace, as men are served by women*
> *Who comfort them in darkness and in sun.*

Oh, honey girl, let's admit it, she thought: she was uneasy,
uneasy. Everything was too weird, time had gotten com-

pletely out of hand lately, dancing all over the place to its own tunes. Howard muttered, rolled again so that she had two inches left to her on the bed. Again he tossed, onto his stomach. A few seconds later, onto his back.

> *And he writes like an antique man of bronze*
> *That is beaten by furies visible . . .*

Sleep was out of the question. She ran the faucet so that she could take two aspirins. Out of the faucet came air. She chewed the pills, but anxiety tightened her throat and she could barely provide the saliva to wash the white dust down. Her mouth sour, she sat on the edge of the bed and scrawled postcards by moonlight. The card faces had photographs, subtitled for NATO consumption, of the Temple of Concord, the Temple of Juno, the sacred ridge with flowering almond, even one with the outstretched stone giant: *Il Telamone, Der Telamon, Le Telamon, The Telamon.* The last she sent off to one of the Three Freaks from school days, writing, "Had picnic all over *him* today, catered by dashing and libidinous natives. Howard fine, me fine, but no one ever sleeps around here except yon fellow, inscrutable and supine."

She wrote with the cards propped on her bare knee, with wrist tucked under to write in the wrong direction, with Howard muttering and tossing at every third word. Her handwriting struck her as worse than ever.

10

INTERNAL combustion, the screeching of a beast, the lop-sided old trundle of cartwheels awakened the Americans. For the third morning, noise rode upon them, or they within the noise. Howard stretched, lapping over the bed at both ends. "Now how," he wanted to know, "does a great heavy cart like that fit in a little old room like this? Six inches of floor space, and every fruit retailer wants in."

Sarah laughed, glad of his mood. It was, after all, a festival day. But there was no sun, and into the claustral gray of their room stole the long sinking morning wail again, that incomprehensible recitative on the price of cauliflowers and the melancholia of commerce, sung by the man with burned face and checkered shirt, whose voice could last an hour without a break for breath, chanting halfway to Africa.

"I see that we're still halfway to Africa," Sarah said.

They arose to lean against the window, in their under-wear. The buying and selling, the roaring and plodding along the gray dust of their street was at a fierce pitch to be over and done with before the celebrations. Below their window a curly man called to his friend. "Eh, Joo-va! Eh, Joo-va!" The friends joined, cursed the sky for a dull and cold misfortune, went off with locked arms for holiday haircuts, elbowing aside vendors and kerchiefed crones. In the ravine across the way, the pile of rotting lemons and orange pulps had grown; but without their glisten of sun, they were unmistakably and simply garbage.

Sarah sighed. "That grocery man seemed awfully picturesque a few days ago. Today I fear he may, he just may, give me a headache." She already had one, of course, a crack in her cerebrum running down to her left eyebrow.

"Sarah. Honey. You could do us both a big favor by not developing a headache today." He was most gentle about it, tired, patient, huge and hovering.

"Oh? Well, I'll try to oblige."

"I'm sorry about last night," he said. "I guess we do better without pagan rites."

"Oh, well. The nights around here just don't seem to work out as well as the days. If they did, when would I write my postcards?" She waved them in triumph. He gave her a friendly hug.

He rummaged through the strewn suitcase for clothes. Their bodies were stale. He felt it unpleasant to be crowded, in underwear, while scuffed light seeped into their cubicle. She still sat on the edge of the bed, half naked and humble.

"Let's spend the morning together," she said.

He was all for it, tossed her clothes to her, told her what an extraordinary place they could go off to see — the sanctuary to the earth gods, made long before the temples, long before, carved into a dark cliff. They could burrow around like moles, really get into the earth, and have plenty of time afterwards for coffee. It was a perfect day for earth gods.

She made no move to dress. "No. I meant just relaxing."

"Here?"

"Here, for a while. If you like burrowing in caves. Or

let's find some peaceful breakfast place. An English Tea
Room, or something."

"English Tea Room!" But he never mocked harshly. He
reminded her that a sanctuary like the one here was something they might never see again in their lives. Something
in them belonged to it. Something that went back into a
common past, before Christians, Greeks, history, headaches.
Didn't she think it might be interesting?

"No! Frankly, Owda my boy, no. I've had it with the
past. Up to here. The more past it is, the more I've had it."
She attacked the guidebook he was tactfully thumbing
through and which she had read so diligently; her headache
dictated the drift. "The past is a crock. Why should I give
three cheers for what anybody did, just as long as it was
two thousand years ago? Were people any better? So
Phalaris was a ruler here and built a big brass bull and
roasted people he didn't like inside it and when they
howled it sounded like a bellow from the bull. Nifty. Clever
ancients. Lord, Eisenhower may be an old windbag, but
he's not as bad as *that!* Nine temples were built here in
eighty years. Okay. They're gorgeous. We've seen them. The
Paris Trib says thirty-four hundred new buildings were
started in New York the first quarter of last year. Okay.
Future historians, start cheering. I'm not comparing them,
Owda. I'm saying sometimes people use the past the way
they use drugs. Especially you. The present is what counts."

"We'll have a lifetime of the present, back home. But
here isn't exactly the place. Is it?" He looked vaguely hurt.

"Don't interrupt when I'm being so brilliant. It's not
even the present that counts. That's a word, like the past.
We count. That's who. What *we* feel and what *we* do.
That's all. That's the whole kit and kaboodle, whatever
the hell that means. So if you want to go out and get high

on your temples and earth gods, go ahead! I'd rather sit and talk to you, or do anything with you. Or with anybody else alive. And if you're going out, then I'd still rather sit. I'll think about me. At least I'm alive."

She felt better already. It wasn't a bad speech for a girl in her underwear. In fact, she was so cheered by it that she was almost ready to jump into her clothes and have a good time archaeologically spelunking with big old Howard.

But the trouble with trying to get a rise out of him was that he always took it so seriously. He stood in his beat-up sweater and khakis, occupying most of the vertical air space in the room, looking ponderously baffled as if all his homework and doing-and-dying for the team and searching for the *summum bonum* had been marked REJECTED.

The sputterings, plosive wheels, hagglings from the street broke around his head. "I could say we are the past," he finally said, "and things like that. But you don't want to hear what I have to say right now, Sarah. I'd better go. You're completely irrational. Have some aspirin and a rest."

"Go ahead," she said, flatly.

"Should I bring back some breakfast?"

"We'll go out when you're back."

The more impossible he had been, bringing it all on, the more hurt he looked when it came. Then she, of course, was in the wrong. Most maddening of all were his heroic efforts at self-control — the behemoth listening to his decent heart and not stampeding; tough-but-oh-so-gentle; wouldn't hurt a fly; nuclear energy harnessed for peaceful purposes.

"Take off, buster," she said.

He gave her an intelligent and forgiving look.

At their keyhole, the daughter of the house made broom noises and burst into song. It was her current favorite, called "Stupidella," and its argument was: what a foolish little thing a certain *she* is, not to know that a certain party loves her. It was a particularly derivative, tinny, whining tune sung in the daughter's particularly thin, scratchy, and wheedling voice, a voice, Sarah had observed yesterday at same hour, same tune, which had all the charm of a postnasal drip. She looked up at Howard to see what a sly wisp of a smile might accomplish, in memory of yesterday's laughter.

Nothing.

"You'll be comfortable with the whole bed to yourself," he said. "I'll be back before the boys get here. We'll all enjoy the Festival. It's in the present."

"Mail my cards on your way out."

Off he went, shoulders rolling, to commune with the chthonic deities.

She was left alone in the gray swill of a morning, with the rattling and rising hysteria of the town in her ears, with "Stupidella" whining outside the door. She beat on her pillow in fury and frustration.

11

THERE was a time when people who took naps were awakened by alarm clocks. Came another time when clocks were replaced by Topolino horns. Sarah, amused by the droll bleat, yawned and stretched, and waited for Howard to tell them something. Bleat-bleat-repeat, beneath their window. She looked about. No Howard. Her head did seem a little better. She held a blanket from the bed shambles over her bosom — as in the movies — and went to the window. The morning was still gray, still seemed in the same stage of activity. Salvatore hopped out of his car, all chivalry amid the tumult.

"Good morning, *signora cara,*" he called up to her. "Forgive the disturbance. But is it possible to offer you and Owda some coffee?"

She said Howard was out being a faithful tourist.

"Oh." Conspiratorial smile. "Well, why don't you come? Unless it would do you better to rest. We'll have a beautiful breakfast."

Why not? Better, by her program, to enjoy the company of two lively boys than to lie around in the absence of one man. She said she would love to, if they could wait a second.

There is something about brushing heavy hair, about the feel of a decent dress after days of squalor, about having a face that doesn't necessarily revolt you in the mirror — Sarah tried out her sly wisp of a smile on herself, and it worked. She felt dazed, from fragmented sleep, but better. She really must try to be nicer to Howard. Solemn old whale. The thing you learned about Howard was that he was so much better than anything he said could lead you to believe. You had to listen to his actions, his dreams, his clear eyes; never his words. Maybe he was even going to be a great man someday. God knows the competition wasn't much, from what she had seen of this world. Anyway, she went downstairs humming a tune she knew — not "Stupidella"— hoping the boys were patient types.

Salvatore was sitting patiently, but alone.

She sidestepped the kinetic chaos of the street, refused to become involved with cauliflowers, or even mandarin oranges, smiled into his window, said, "Where's Pietro?"

He looked disappointed that she sounded disappointed. "Oh, he's down in my shop, finishing a piece of work for me. We'll go pick him up. You might take a look at my workshop, if that would interest you."

Why not?

Salvatore was gracious, helping her in. He was in a blue suit with pencil stripes, not cut so well as the town dandies liked, but he himself looked so scrubbed and well hewn that he more than compensated. Apparently he was not going to be naughty today, so if he didn't mention yesterday's jockeying, she wouldn't either.

They cruised the gray streets (not cutting the ignition this time), and chatted about the party, Sarah giving emphatic assurances that she had enjoyed every insane bit of it.

He said that the Uncle was much taken with her, had talked for an hour of her intelligence, litheness, beauty.

Sarah had no objections to that.

He stared straight ahead. At length he brought them

down the street where the dancing beneath Polifemo had taken place in the first twilight. Then he stopped the car in his abrupt way.

The street was quiet in the clouded daylight, almost bucolic, with strewings of hay, mixed animal and gasoline scents. She remembered with an eerie pang the crying of the sheep and donkeys just beyond the wall at dusk, the monster's red eye glaring high in the headlights.

"Would you like to see where we work, then?" He was gazing at her carefully.

He helped her out.

The neighborhood was in a lull, but the houses had the look, and the smells, of much dressing and cooking going on inside. Through gaps in the wall, the hills faded into the dull sky with dots of stone cottages scattered miles apart from each other.

She had trouble negotiating the rutted alley in her heels. He teased her, saying that Sicilian girls were mountain goats, even in spiked shoes.

The door of his stone shed was ajar. As they went in he called, "Pietro! Pietro! Eh, little saint, where are you?"

There were deep histories of grease on the packed dirt floor, but the place was astonishingly neat and well swept. There was a long low table, very clean, with specifications, manuals, orders, pencils, all in place; wrenches and tools hung along the walls according to type and size. There were engine diagrams tacked to a tar paper side wall, and one picture — where an Illinois mechanic would have had his girlie calendar. It was the portrait by the much-beloved Antonello da Messina of the Virgin reading before the Annunciation, her face beneath a modest cowl, calm, intelligent, deeply meditative. Sarah gave a gasp of admiration at the whole effect of the life lived here.

"My studio," said Salvatore. His eyes suddenly clouded over. "I believe, whatever it is a human being can do, no matter how insignificant, it must be done with the best that is within him. The best! There is no other truth about work." He gave no embarrassed laugh, as she automatically expected, but touched his breast again with his dark fingers.

Sarah was fascinated. Where did some men find this kind of concern?

He fell into his old arguments again, said that German and American mechanics were so famous, but they relied on materials, had no imagination. Give an Italian mechanic a picture of any good engine in the world, and his two hands, his head, a wrench were enough to solve its problems. He said engines were beautiful because you always knew where you stood with them. Not like the weather, not like people. It was a great comfort to him . . .

Sarah nodded. She was glad to have glimpsed the concern in him, after such concentrated exposure to his short legs, his vanities, his little games.

He said Pietro must be working somewhere out behind.

While he went through a side door into the garage — glimpses of small cars in various surgical stages there — she gazed out the window toward the cacti and stones of the ravine in back. Such force, in this meager shed at the edge of a poor town, at the edge of an island, at the edge of Europe . . .

He was back. "Pietro has escaped, evidently. And the job isn't done." He made a gesture of despair. "*Beh*, depend on a friend . . ."

He looked out the window with her. A lightening on the hills, a hint of breakthrough for the sun. "But, it is Festival." Pale-eyed resignation.

"Yes," she said with a soft smile. "It's a festival day. Let's forgive all our friends."

"Even our new friends, Sara?"

"*Especially* our new friends."

In testimony to this, Salvatore collected a small kiss from her lips. She gave it willingly, as part of a nostalgic ritual of girlhood — the little kiss to the nice boy after a date. (Then, "Thanks again. It was a lovely evening," and one popped in through the front door, leaving venery out in the cold.)

"That was pleasant," Salvatore said. His eyes were clear, amused.

"Well, it is Festival."

Accordingly, he helped himself to another sweet sip from her lips. This one, too, she gave. The ritual provided a second, ungrudging kiss for the boy who had been especially nice, or generous, or somehow meritorious.

Salvatore had a hand on her breast, in violation of several intervening rituals. Amusement was fading from his eyes.

She moved toward a gentle dislodgement. She didn't want condemnations, embarrassments.

He squeezed with more nuance. With both hands now, he squeezed and caressed her breasts.

"No, really, Salvatore. Turridu! You're making a mistake."

She pushed at his wrists, which were wrists that could toss an axle into the air, and catch it again. She moved to back away, but she was already against the work table. ("That'll teach you, to dabble in flirtations with a smoldering Latin," and she collected her energies for the big No.)

"*Ma, bellezza mia!*" He had let her seize his arms away but then he locked them behind her, along with her own arms, bending her in the shape of a question mark back over the table. He kissed her neck, her ear, bit at her lobe. "Salvatore! Damn it!"

But before she had recognized the event, it was almost too late. He was upon her with fierce power, a man almost hysterical with momentum. He was pressing her back upon the table, clamping her with his shoulders and knees, even using his head like a bull, kissing her everywhere with his sandpaper face. She saw all her mistakes, in flashes. In seconds she wouldn't be able to stop him. No hope against the brunt of nature in him. Nor in her. He had bunched her dress upward, was forcing her legs below, pouring his torrent of Sicilian words upon her. But Christ! She wasn't a beast! Her arms buckled when she tried to push. Then, kick him between the legs. But she couldn't be that vicious. And his legs were already within hers, forcing. She screamed *Stop Stop Stop Stop Stop,* banged at the back of his neck. He pulled his head back, astounded. His eyes were blinded flares like a racer's lights in the night. He hit her in the face, quite hard. Oh no, oh no, she whimpered. She was only human. Don't let him hit me again. Please. He did. She fell apart. She yielded with him at first in horror at herself, but she was willing, and then she was away, riding off among lunar valleys, part of her in the center gliding, yielding, all the rest nowhere, until into nowhere came her own voice, in gasps, "Turridu! Turridu!"

She was out of control. Her body shook with rag doll violence. He tried to smooth her face, her hair, with his rough hands. Then he pulled at his own sandy hair, trying not to be frantic. He went again to the door. "There's no one," he said. "There's no one." She sobbed again, and again. She couldn't believe it. "But why did you come

here?" he repeated. "Why did you arrange not to be with
Owda? Why didn't you give a sign of no, before it was too
late? Why? Why?"

She was unable to say anything, without losing control
again. He helped her to neaten herself, gave her a chair by
the window so that she wouldn't have to look at him for
a while. She watched blots of sunlight beginning to rove
the hills.

Quiet came. She did not want to blame a man who had
been generous, whose life was hard, whom she had misled.
She supposed she would get over the trauma. Put it all
down to experience. He stood, remorsefully. He did not
want to accuse her of tempting him, because she had not,
not in the local way with words or eyelashes. It was only
by being what she was, by being lenient, by laughing, by
having the legs she had, and round hips, and the honey
that had to be tasted. Then they sat silently, on chair and
worktable. Part of her dress had been soiled, by a mark of
grease on the table. She worked on it. They were both
much sobered. She was studying the swamps of carelessness
within her; he, his demon. He was still touched by her
lack of accusation, yet life had disappointed him. Either
she should have been grateful, or she should have shown
him ahead of time that she wouldn't be.

"Sara," he said. "You were not made to wander the
world. You should stay home, have children."

"Thanks, hey," she said, in English.

She didn't explain.

He got her back to his car when no one was in the street
to see them, skillfully dropped her off amid traffic some
blocks from her house, did everything to protect her.

(But earlier in the raucous street with vendors and
heaped lemons, everyone had seen them go off together.

And behind windows in his quiet neighborhood, many had seen the two arrive, walk down the alley, and return only later in the motley sunlight.)

12

Howard was walking alone beneath the clearing sky, which was a state of things he had much desired during the past three days, but he was troubled.

For one thing, he wasn't truly alone. He had his knot of scamps with him, flitting around his legs, piping, playing over and over again their single hilarious game. He had acquired the first three as he passed the fringe of town toward the glowering cliff which held the sanctuary. As soon as they saw him, they had given up their cat hunt, or whatever was their previous engagement, to come running. They were tattered boys; he gave them a few lire, feeling guilty and foolish as always. They withdrew for a conference. After he had taken five more strides under the sullen sky, trying to find the mood fit for a visit to the oldest gods, there was a scampering at his side and a tapping on his pants leg. He stopped. Down there, wanting to talk to him, was surely the champion scamp of the world, who wore a threadbare Ike jacket with the sleeves cut away, and apparently nothing else. His face was dark and tiny, even for his body, and from snapping eyes to kneecaps and filthy fingertips he thrummed with a metabolism all his own, like a bird's. Howard smiled down. The champion cupped his hand about his mouth to make sure his voice would carry through the interminable wastes of atmosphere until it reached Howard's ear, and he shouted, *"Fa freddo lassù?* Is it cold up there?"

"Up where?" Howard said.

The champion's face tightened up into a walnut. He was unable to bear the excruciations of his own wit. "Up there! Up there!" He pointed. He meant around Howard's head. His friends died.

"No," the American laughed. *"È normale.* It's just normal. Here, I'll show you." He bent over and reached out with an arm as long as the boy's body, but that was one ride the champ wasn't taking.

The three followed close behind him. All the way to the cave's entrance, they squealed tirelessly, *"Fa freddo lassù?* Is it cold up there? Is it cold up there?" and laughed each time with the fresh glory of it.

When he emerged, blinking beneath the breaking sky, they had gone. But somehow on a lower street they picked him up again, with reinforcements. They wouldn't leave him. They piped their refrain, and piped it again, and again, swarming, "Is it cold up there?" never getting too close or too far, never needing the least variation to recoup their hilarity.

Howard couldn't let himself be angered at a boys' game (nor at boys who were held together with clothespins and woolen patches). But any hint of humiliation had always enraged him. Now he sensed ominously that the townspeople along the way were perceiving him only as a big blond joke.

The scamps were small models of the town, as he had come to feel it, crowding, nipping, yapping about his (or anyone's) lower parts. He resented it bitterly. Not that he demanded to be seen as lofty, or felt himself to be so, but all he wanted from this place was that his head be left free to follow a few trains of thought, his eyes and memory be given space to re-create a sense of time, now, before it was too late, a sense of the ancient rolling of time and all men's place in it, from which he could draw energy, relevance, solace in the pressure pot of American cities which cooked people only in the present, allowed nothing else. But this place was its own little pot.

"Is it cold up there?"

And Sarah had not been a help. She had a quick wit, a wonderful body; he still loved her, of course; she could be the world's best companion when she wanted to be. But he did not understand her. If the wind blew from the north one day, she would head south. If it changed the next day, she would turn with it. It was all the same to her — this town, or the Doric temples, or the wives' auxiliary at the Officers' Club. Everything passed through her. She was a sieve. Nothing stuck, she had no sense of trying to find a structure, to make a structure of her life. And because he wanted to make some kind of structure in his few years on this earth, she resented him. Because he wanted to contribute, she ridiculed him. She had come here, but only to humor him for what she considered his whims, not to seek anything. And she didn't even mean her wild attack on the past this morning. All she meant was that she had a headache. If they were to have a sunny morning tomorrow on a soft, grassy hillside near the temples, she would say, "You know what, Owda? Let's deck the mangy modern world. Build us a lean-to here and we'll live on nuts and fish and think about those darling old Greeks going up in their bed sheets to pray." He could hear her voice, and it gave him a terrible pang. Even the way she had accepted him as Owda. If those boys told her to come to the Festival dressed as an owl, she would.

"Is it cold up there? Is it cold up there?"

He had shrugged off the nag of circumstance when he faced that cliffside, hanging over the stream bed, a dark reminder of the age and awesomeness of this earth, and he had crouched double into the corners of the rock-hewn rooms to breathe the deep bruit coolness, to remember that men not so different from himself had cringed there in terror lest the corn goddess be angry with them, had crept further toward the heart of her earth and carved elaborate conduits for the rock water to flow, purifying. But it hadn't worked for Howard. It was too remote. He couldn't possibly feel any part of himself at home there. He came out into the air, which is what he craved, and saw the slow sweep of the land. But then, walking back among the close walls, roofs, outside drainpipes of the town, he felt ever less at home.

Observing nothing that surrounded him now, not even aware that the piping boys had scampered away, Howard mused again on trying to be at home in the world. Not the least doubt about it: for him, home was where tall fluted columns stood above the sea, where waves opened scrolls of light and memory below . . .

Then he stood, stupefied by his dream from last night. The shore; and behind him, a forest of stone columns. A little man next to him has a face he hasn't seen in years, with a smile meant to soothe him. "Hi," the little man says, "I'm the quarterback. Okay?" That seems settled and they go off together for a long swim, keeping long, long, even strokes in tandem. It is the sea, but it spreads before them without resistance like an unbounded luminous lake. They swim always into the glaze of sun, with a great sense of well-being. Howard turns to the quarterback to express pleasure in this, but the other's face is strained, he snarls, and it is clear that they are now racing. Howard does not want to race. He says so, over and over, but the grace and well-being are gone and he begins to swim with churning, rolling, desperate strokes . . .

"Signor Otorn! Signor Otorn!"

It was the Uncle. Surroundings returned. A peeling ochre wall in a patch of sunlight; a butcher's window with red lollops hanging from hooks, trays heaped white with honeycomb tripe; a news booth where uncle had been perusing the slicks: *Sud, Meridiano, Oggi, Epoca, Gente, Il Reporter, Confidenze, Sportmondo, Bella, Eva.* And lottery and auto-race posters; some men still in black, belted raincoats despite the sun; Vespas cruising; girls with flowers in their hair and in their arms; flies; bodies scurrying home topped with last-minute groceries instead of heads, wrapped in newspaper leaves; a busful of Germans, singing; two priests arguing acidly; a boy hefting a tray with stone-sized loaves of bread, having trouble squeezing past Howard; Uncle and the newsdealer eying him.

They shook hands, wished each other *buona festa.* Uncle said, "I was afraid for a moment that my party had caused you to be paralyzed."

"Not at all," laughed Howard. "I'm often outside myself, somewhere. It's my affliction."

"Ah, I know it well, this affliction. How often I myself stand, recalling other days, happier possibilities."

Uncle had taken his arm and they strolled along, Howard measuring his steps to keep time with a waddle. Uncle had relied this morning on yesterday's pre-party shave; seedings of gray marred his round pinkness. His black suit showed erosions in the sunlight.

Coffee was offered, as a matter of course. Howard said he should get back to see Sarah, whose head had not lasted as well as his after the indulgences of yesterday. But Uncle persuaded him to wait ten minutes: "You cannot imagine, signor Otorn, the pleasure of finding an intelligent foreigner to help one pass the time."

In the bar mirror, below the AUTOVOX calendar, Howard saw how fuzzily his own pale need for a shave was showing, how his cheekbones had reddened from the picnic sun, how broad, conspicuous, and bad his old sweater looked among the careful suits. He'd have to compensate by courtesy.

"Did you converse with my wife last night?" Uncle asked.

Howard said he was sorry, but no; so much had gone on.

"You're fortunate. She has nothing up here." Uncle tapped his head with pudgy forefinger. "Absolutely nothing. To try to converse with my wife is to experience despair."

The American couldn't discover courtesy either in agreeing or disagreeing. He sipped his coffee.

"You and your *signora* are both intelligent. You have interests that are shared. You can talk seriously, like human beings. You can make complicated jokes to each other."

Howard agreed; that was so.

"But my wife is as empty as this cup. I'll tell you frankly, when I came back from the war, I was very distraught. No work. Everything in great disorder. I seduced this young girl, beautiful, shy. Miraculous body. Then I was afraid her family would kill her. You see how it is here. I married her, out of pity. Most men wouldn't have done it. I don't brag — that was simply my one act of virtue, in a whole life. We had a pleasant month, then sixteen years of boredom. She is ignorant beyond belief, and do you know the one ambition of my life now?"

Howard waited.

Uncle put his hand on his companion's great arm. "Since divorce is impossible, it is to become a driver on one of those touristic autobus lines that circle the island. The Golden Ribbon, you know — Palermo, Cefalù, Siracusa, Taormina, Messina. That way I could meet educated foreigners, like you and the signora Otorn, and be away from home four days at a time. Is that not a pathetic ambition for a man of self-respect? But what is there to do? And in the meantime, I grow fatter."

In unison, they drained their cups of sugar and dregs.

Howard would have preferred not to see the man expose himself. The style just wasn't his. He would much rather hear how last night's skit came about — was it passed from father to son? For millenia? But when it came to a test, he couldn't get himself to ask questions like an anthropologist tracking down the natives' customs. Nearby, two men broke into vicious laughter, apparently at a Neapolitan folk song from the jukebox. He did ask about that.

"Ah, there is much resentment here against Naples. *Ancora due caffè, ragazzino!* The North ridicules the Neapolitans for being wild and dishonest. They cannot deny it, so they come down here to laugh at us for being wild and dishonest. But we are not. We are just poor, warm people — limited." The two fresh cups arrived.

"I could tell you such things, signor Otorn, if time only allowed. Yes. Ah yes. In literature — do you like literature? — they always write of the heart, the heart, the heart. Everyone believes it. But in this world, intelligence is the only light. Without it, there is no light." He turned his sad moonface up to Howard, desperate to show that in his eyes, at least, the light was there. "You and your wife have it. And you have opportunity. You must enrich it, travel everywhere, come to know the world. You will be

most fortunate. But here, even with intelligence . . . Take
my nephew, for example. Salvatore. He could have been an
engineer, a constructor of new cities; and even his little
friend, Pietro — that was a boy intended by nature to be a
poet, a musician. He sang in the choir like an angel. But
. . ." Eloquence, in the gestures of his hands.

Again, Howard nodded. (He had made that very point
to Sarah, as they were laying out the glowing pimentos
and cheeses on *il gigante*, yesterday. She had answered,
"Oh, they're decent lads, all right. But let's not overdo the
mute inglorious Milton bit.")

"But my nephew had to support his whole family — six
women — for years. So he lost his eduction. His father was
killed, you know, in the war. Not far from this town."

Howard had a sudden guess to make, with troubled
heart. "Tell me one thing. If you don't mind. Salvatore's
father . . . he was killed by the Americans, wasn't he?"

"Oh, I'm surprised that he told you. Turridu never
talks of it, normally. A very closed boy. Let us say, a bomb
from the war killed the father. He was a fine man, not so
intelligent as his son, perhaps, but of a more sweet temperament. He was . . . well, you understand, my brother."

"I am deeply sorry. I want you to know that." Speaking
a foreign language seemed more a confinement than ever
to Howard, just then.

"Ah, signor Otorn." Uncle gripped his arm again. "What
do you and I have to do with whom the governments let
their bombs fall upon?"

(This, too, he had discussed with Sarah, after a night
of war talk in Rome. Again, she had spoken almost as if
it were a "bit," with a quote about "wetting right many
a nipperkin," which he had not been able to place or

grasp. She, so anxious to have it all roll off her back; he, to make it all into his own structure.)

Uncle broke the embarrassed silence. "And did you have the occasion to converse with Francesca last night?"

Howard said he had; she seemed an attractive and energetic girl.

"That, she is. Can you imagine, her parents were going to take her home in anger at the beginning of the party, because she was dancing too close with you?"

"No, I can't! I mean, that's very hard to imagine."

"Well, there you have it. Francesca wants to be a modern girl. She's had some education, she reads, she wants to have her own views. But do you know what the difference is between her views and her parents'? A thousand years. *Ecco,* that's the difference. Salvatore has been courting her, more or less, for ten months, because he considers her worthy of respect, perhaps, but he has not yet had the chance to be alone with her, not even for one minute. You can imagine how he feels."

Howard thought he could.

"Since her twelfth birthday she has never been allowed to appear alone on the streets of this town. Not once. She is afraid to break the customs, afraid of what the town would do, so she is cruel to her parents instead. She could go north, find work, but instead she sits at home, and they have war. You foreigners come here in torrents, with your own free lives, and you never see what life is like behind these windows. You should read the letter columns in the women's magazines. You would see ten thousand miserable stories, lives of fine intelligent girls ruined forever by fear, ignorance, old superstitions . . . I was reading them myself at the newsstand. There was one from a girl who is in love with a fine boy. He has a job, wants to marry, but she had rheumatic fever when she was younger, and she has a sister who was abandoned by her husband. So now she thinks there are two reasons why it is impossible for her ever to marry. That's the one I was reading when we met. I was afraid you had caught me."

Howard looked at his watch. It was after eleven.

The uncle said he was sorry to have detained him for so long. Of course, he must hurry off to his wife, help ease her headache, help her enjoy the Festival. He must realize what a blessing it was from the gods, to have a Sara, so intelligent, gracious, beautiful.

"Take care of her always," said Uncle. "For my sake." He held his hand to his heart.

Howard was touched, surprisingly. He made a frantic effort to pay for the second round of coffee.

"No, no, signor Otorn," Uncle said, reproachfully. When they shook hands, tears came to his eyes. *"Per bacco,* it repays me a thousand times to have the honor of passing the time with a splendid person like you, to hear your views on life . . ."

The dark eyes in the bar studied their farewell scene. Who in town did not recognize the blond American giants by now?

13

Howard was out in the riotous streets. Festival spirit was building pressure. Headway was hard. He felt rushed, behind, confined again. But he smiled briefly: what *were* his views on life? It was just as well that Uncle hadn't dredged anything out of him, this particular morning.

And yet, a strange sense had come out to him from these compressed days, from the pouring out of people about their lives. The desire, the fierce desire of every person not to be negligible . . .

A tall man, drunk and staggering, with a rust-colored beard, tried to stop him, talking some Scandinavian language. Scamps clung at the heels of two Africans in bright robes, shouted, *"Guarda i neri!* Look at the blacks! Look at the blacks!"

Howard broke into a trot, then into a broken-field run through the thronged streets.

When he reached the front of their house, he was in a sweat, and yet there was a coldness on his skin. He hadn't eaten since the picnic. In the sun that poured from a sky almost free of clouds, he saw Sarah talking to Pietro.

The mild boy, who had sung like an angel in the choir, stepped aside to let the spouses greet in private.

She was in her blue dress (she called it her "Michelin

one-star dress"), with high heels, lipstick, hair brushed into
a rich cumulus. She clung to his shoulders for a moment.

"Oh Howard, I'm so glad to see you!"

"That's the surprise of the day." He kissed her happily,
on the lips.

A passerby applauded. Pietro shouted something at him.
The man laughed.

"Oh really, really, Howard! So glad! I thought I had
done myself in, with that moronic argument this morning.
I was sure you'd run off to sea, or eloped with the corn
goddess, or something. I wouldn't have blamed you." She
kissed his sweatered shoulder. "And look what I found on
our doorstep — an abandoned waif!" She led him behind
a pluck of the sleeve toward Pietro.

Hectic and apologetic: rare styles for Sarah.

Pietro's black suit, black hair, shoes, skin were all
brushed and polished to the bone.

"*Buona festa,* Pietro!"

"*Buona festa, caro* Owda!"

They shook hands, Sarah clinging to his free arm.

Pietro said, "I was supposed to do some work for Turridu
early this morning. But I thought to myself, I shall have
work all my life. At least, I hope so." He laughed, sadly,
and they made encouraging noises. "But when again shall
I have such friends as you? Never, never, I said to myself.
And so I came over as soon as I could, in the hope of
offering you some coffee. But it was so quiet in your window, and I did not want to disturb. I know we have forced
too much to do upon you. I sat and sat, and I began to be
afraid that you would sleep through the Festival. Then at
last I saw a vision approaching me from down the hill. It
was Sara! And then, less than a minute later, I see you
coming the same way. I am very content."

Pietro had determined to fill the air all day with words, in case there had been, or was about to be, trouble. One can never tell.

"Oh?" Howard said to Sarah. "You were out?"

"Yes, for a while." Sarah paused. (They would have to go over the whole business, of course, in an open, rational way. But why right now? She hated the thought of dragging everyone through her mess, on a day of festival. The outgoing train would do, for a long talk.) "I was starved, so I went out for some breakfast. I hope you didn't wait all this time, to have something."

"Well, I met Salvatore's uncle by accident and we had some coffee. Also a long conversation."

"Conversation!" said Pietro, with a glint. "I doubt that you said ten words."

Howard admitted that his Italian wasn't up to expressing anything very interesting.

"Your Italian? It would be all the same if you both were speaking Chinese. No one ever gets ten words in with the Uncle. For that, he is famous. He has lost the use of his ears."

Sharpness from Pietro: Also an unusual style.

Sarah was clinging still, to Howard's arm. She rubbed her cheek against his shoulder. He chuckled. "It was pretty strange. Afterwards, he told me how glad he was to have my views on life."

"The Uncle has not listened to anyone's views on anything for twenty years. If you are ever unfortunate enough to be riding on his bus, he will tell you where you want to go, and why."

Sarah said, "You should not hold last night so much against him, Pietro. It really wasn't that important."

"Perhaps. But I am pleased at least that he gave Owda some coffee. We won't have to lose time trying to eat. The crowds are impossible, everywhere. Insane."

The Americans accepted this and accepted, therefore, even hollower stomachs for the day, a condition for which a life of milk and steaks had not prepared them.

Howard said, "I'll run inside and change into a suit. I'm a disaster, next to you two." He felt his beard and the cooling perspiration that streaked it, felt his rumpled hair, indicated the floppy khaki tubes on his legs, the sneakers.

But Pietro said he looked fine — had he seen some of the other foreigners this morning? Short leather pants, beards a meter in length, striped bathrobes — everything. And they had almost no time to find Salvatore before the processions began.

Howard looked doubtful.

"Owda, what difference could it make? I assure you that you are the most impressive man this town has ever seen, just as you are."

Sarah said, "Oh, it's true! I'm sure it's true!" She squeezed his hand.

He looked at her strangely.

Pietro took his other arm and they marched off into the crowds, which were becoming impossible and insane, everywhere.

But the real insanity, Pietro said, would only begin in the night. Now it was just crowds and shouting and the floats and music, but after dark, people threw wine into themselves, threw confetti at everyone else, and old fruit, anything. Tons of junk. The town looked like an artillery raid during a snowfall. Lately they had begun to sell hard rubber balls on elastic strings — did he make himself understood? — so that they could be bounced off heads, particularly foreigners', particularly girls', and then brought back again. They hurt cruelly.

Sarah said, "I can't picture you doing that, Pietro. Festival or no Festival."

"I don't. That is, I don't like to. But everyone does it. Even Salvatore loves to. He says it releases one's true feelings. I can't agree." He leaned close to both of them. "I can't agree with anything here. Even with my dearest friends."

While they were leaning close, Sarah asked him whether he really had had a job to do for Salvatore, which should have been finished that morning. In the workshop.

"Ah Sara, don't accuse me. I'm grateful to Turridu for finding me pieces of work. But what difference does it make if it finishes a day late? It's only a . . . a thing. But I wanted to be with you two."

"Oh. Well, that's very nice."

In the surge and color and noise, Howard had lost the relevance of the conversation.

They were working their way down a narrow street. Houses, shops, trattorias, all were closed and emptied. All heads were out under the sun. Music clanged up from the center. Donkeys tethered in secrecy joined the howling; the last cars pinioned in the streets claxoned with despair. Sarah picked carefully among the cobblestones in her high heels, with both men offering hands to guide now, and with much necessary high swaying of her rear parts, as when a horse steps steeply downhill. Remarks were passed on the subject, from behind. Pietro turned to glare, and Howard joined him, without having caught the words. The remarks subsided into the many-faced uproar, then resumed

as soon as they turned front again. Rolls of colored paper
sailed.

They emerged into the square where the young policeman's white gloves had been spiraling on the day of
arrival, and it was in glorious sun with much brilliance
of raw concrete and with the palm-tree tops inaudible,
whether because of little wind or because the human surge
today would suffuse their scrapings even in a gale. A band
of Polish dancers in braids and costumes — Pietro shouted
that there would be an exhibition of dance at the temples
— was trying to fight through the crowds to get somewhere,
but men circled them, laughing, shouting "Do a polka! Do
a polka!" Howard distinctly heard a familiar chirrup of
voices from somewhere out of the chaos: "Is it cold up
there? Is it cold up there?" He didn't feel offended. In fact,
he turned his head about and smiled above the dark bob-
bing crush, in search of the scamp in Ike jacket, as if he
had something he wanted to discuss with him. Then he
became aware that he was acting, feeling, very, very
strangely.

There is a strangeness that children know, when the
night is deep, but they fight to stay awake. They are awake,
yet part of the world is suddenly missing, or one of their
eyes or ears has gone somewhere, or half a head has been
misplaced. Distances change; walls, lamps and pictures
begin marching, and yet a reach of the hand and everything
is where it was. That strangeness is forgotten, until drink,
illness, other such confusions bring something akin — a
floating. Howard felt this now, that his head floated above
a hurling world from which one dimension had with great
skill been extracted. Words and colors sailed up to him,
but he could take them or not, as he wished, like balloons.

If he just let them sail by, they would drift into the absent dimension and no one would know the difference. He laughed at the thought.

Pietro-Sarah said, "Beg pardon, Owda, what's up, Howard?"

"Nothing, nothing. Just the Festival."

At an appointed place, they exchanged fervent handclasps with Salvatore, his mama and various sisters, Uncle and his family, cool Francesca and her parents. Amid the milling, poor Pietro caught a look that passed between Sarah and Salvatore. His face went taut. He stepped up between them, gave them both a quick, agonized glance.

Curiouser and curiouser, Sarah told herself. She had detached herself from the day, decided to let it all be spectacle. But someone seemed to be speeding the film; she wasn't sure she could keep track.

Francesca grasped Howard's hand for an instant; again she gave him a look of appraisal that was surely reserved, as a rule, for objects. She dropped his hand but held him carefully with her eyes, saying, "Perhaps there is something you should know, signor Otorn. Perhaps there is something I should tell you." Howard bent his head more closely, but Pietro was abruptly between them, dragging him off.

"Let's begin our walk, Owda."

Howard was going to protest. But then he was amused. This was without doubt the first time he had ever been blocked out of a play by a one-hundred-and-ten-pounder.

The entire town seemed convinced that if he got within six inches of Francesca he would gobble her up in one bite.

In public. He laughed aloud and wanted to tell Sarah something about it, but her head was beyond Salvatore's and Pietro's, and furthermore she threw him a glance as if he were addled.

Perhaps he was. He had the impression that most of the crowd squeezing into the curved street was working up its festive mood by laughing at him. But he had felt the burn of ridicule ever since the first night in the jukebox cafe, and anyway, if they liked to laugh, it was their privilege. The privilege of the underprivileged. The least they should be allowed. He had been dragooned today into appearing for the public dressed as one of the annual foreign clowns, so he would have to play it out, along with rusty-bearded Swedes and bathrobed Africans. But he would gladly have parted with six inches of his body's height until he left this island. He confronted a knot of faces that mocked openly up at him, from a doorway. Make it ten inches.

Conversation among the four was impossible. They were all victims of a noise storm. Trumpets and drums from the side streets, thunderous amplifications from the cafes, mounting crowd rumbles, and just ahead of them, a riot. The police were trying to butt a path through for the floats. The first had already begun to roll, at the far end. The crowd was avid for battle. It swallowed shiny policemen like bonbons.

Whistles. Arms waving. Hoots.

"*Signore, signori,* please! Please! ! ! The parade must pass!"

United, jolly, roaring front.

Sarah: trying to shout up into his ear something about the way he rolls when he walks.

Salvatore: saying they should get out of this bedlam until the parade begins.

Pietro: responding with enthusiasm, taking Howard's arm.

Pietro said they could watch the last floats getting ready on the south side. He knew where their Polifemo would be.

Sarah preferred to see a different one.

Howard said, true. They knew Polifemo already; his novelty was gone.

They pushed across current, Howard leading the interference, and followed an alley southward between crippled walls until it dropped down a few stairs into an open cobbled *piazzetta* at the edge of the hill on which the town perched. One of the tableau floats was there, in dress rehearsal, with a small and rollicking crowd beneath it, calling encouragement. At the far edge of the square two boys played at pushing each other off the low stone wall. Beyond, the steep drop fell away.

The temples were silhouetted against the wide sea in the distance. Pale rose eruptions of almond swept the valleys.

"Oh, this is charming!" Sarah said. "Ravishing!" She felt the hollowness within her of anxiety, hunger, vestiges of this morning's butting. She hoped to combat it all with adjectives.

The sun beat down upon the scene in the dust of the little square. It sharpened the southern browns and ochres of the slope-roofed houses around the space and fired into incandescence the greens and the soil of the valley below the open side. Any of the typical floats, except Polifemo and his dancers, could have been in preparation here

(there would be a prize for the most artful): the shepherds'
camp with mournful flute, three sheep, and a pot of *ricotta*
bubbling away over a fire; the fishermen's float with nets
being mended amid ancient chants; any of the competing
tarantella teams.

As it turned out, they had stumbled upon another
standby — the mock *vendetta* scene. On the platform the
only props were the doorway to a peasant's cottage, built
against a frame that leaned in turn against the truck cab,
and a tree of papier-mâché. An old man sat by himself on
a corner of the platform, playing accompaniments on a
shrill pipe while the three performers went through their
actions in slow motion, frozen into tableaux at the suit-
ably melodramatic moments. First, the husband and wife,
dressed as peasants, hold hands and gaze into each other's
eyes with decent, happy love: freeze. Applause and irony
from the onlookers. Then husband dons cap and goes off
with crook over his shoulder, pausing to wave to wife, who
waves prettily back: freeze.

Salvatore shouted, *"Brava, brava, Silvana!"* To Howard
and Sarah he explained that she was his cousin ("like
most of the population, you know").

But the others in the square were hooting warnings at
husband, because the villain was also frozen, leering around
the other side of the papier-mâché tree.

Villain, too, is in the knee breeches of a peasant, but he
wears a slick black vest, curlicued Spanish mustaches, and
earrings of gold. He holds his finger to his lips, which makes
the audience hoot more loudly. Then he whispers and flat-
ters the young wife into a lightninglike seduction, to the
moment when she is in his arms, her eyes ablaze with ardor
and fear: freeze.

They were masterful hams. Men and boys in their dark suits cheered in delight. There was an exchange of reminders that *la donna* is like that; the woman doesn't exist who can be trusted out of your sight. The ladies in the impromptu audience giggled and blushed.

But lo! Husband is back, wielding a silvery theatrical knife perhaps two feet long, his face distorted beyond recognition with jealousy and wrath: freeze. Then he raises the knife, which flares in the sun, races at villain, who somehow further curls his mustache with contempt and reaches for his own knife, as young wife shrinks back in anguish: freeze.

This time the square burst into a tumult of participation:

"Bravo for *il cornuto* — the horned one!"

"Run him through, the *bricconaccio!*"

"No, cut off her ear!"

"Eliminate them both!"

There were to be several more tableaux to settle the outcome, but the signal came for the float to take its place, and so the truck driver let out the clutch with a jolt that almost sent the cast flying off the tail end. They waved and blew kisses to the onlookers, who laughed and threw coins after them for a joke and then dispersed, to see the parade.

The entire drama had been run off in less than two minutes, as it would have to be done over and over again along the main street, with musical interludes, and after it withdrew, Howard, Sarah, Pietro, Salvatore had stood perhaps ten seconds too long, frozen silent. They looked about the sunny emptying square. They were almost alone.

Howard shifted on his feet.

Pale-eyed Salvatore looked at him askance. When their eyes met, mockery played.

Sarah began to quip to Pietro, saw *his* eyes, fell silent. Pietro kicked at a cobblestone.

At last, Salvatore said, to Howard, "How did you like the little play?"

"Well, they did a nice job. But melodrama never appealed to me, particularly." Courtesy, as always; as always, truthfulness.

Sarah took his arm. "Me neither," she said.

In Pietro's eyes, part of the dark storm cleared. He asked his old friend, with a voice of mischief, "How did *you* like it?"

"Me?" The sturdy man took a breath, smiled. "Me. Well, I'll tell you frankly, my friends. I think it was a stupid piece of business, backward, a waste of time, like almost everything here. On the other hand, I say that's the way life is, the way we'll always be, so why not show it?"

They stared at him, in degrees of puzzlement. He seemed puzzled at himself, ran fingers through his sandy hair, glanced about the square, which was emptied of all but dust and sunlight now, and the two scamps playing along the wall.

When no one filled the pause, Salvatore-Turridu announced, "But none of you can understand this." He glowered at them, as if he wanted to be challenged. Sarah nodded her head thoughtfully, but the other two refused to show any feeling.

Howard threw off Sarah's arm. His fair face was set, careful.

Abruptly, they all began talking. It was Pietro who made himself heard with suggestions that they really should get over now to see the parade, they really should, it was the only good part of Festival, they wouldn't find a place if they didn't hurry, he knew where the others would be, out the other end of the square, they could find a place with them, with the Uncle, and Francesca, and the others, and if not, then they could go farther down still, but only if they hurried.

Past the floating blur of windows, streamers, faces, Howard made every effort not to suspect that he suspected what he did suspect. There was war within him. He raged against battalions of cocky small men. All his life they had nipped, cut and clipped at him, to bring him down, to subvert. He had held himself in check, and they had lived to poison him through his weakness. Sarah, Sarah, casual Sarah was where he was weak, soft, she was his weakness; he couldn't believe that she would betray him, would let all softness out to be probed in raw daylight; it had never even occurred to him before, never. His fantasies turned red, he squashed battalions, but still he tried to hold himself in check. Salvatore . . . the war . . . poverty . . . justice. But unbidden sources pumped a flow of curious pictures into his mind, curious suggestions, hints of conspiracy, questions.

He did not look at Sarah.

Pietro's voice was producing words, without cease.

Their arrival among the others made a stir. It was a lull between floats; Howard became the next float. Uncle had commandeered the steps before a souvenir shop for his group, and when the Americans stepped up into a prominence of sun there was open laughter. A voice, not a child's, said, "Is it cold up there?" Others picked it up. Howard's face burned. The next band was making its way down, with cymbal clash and piercing cornets. Tumult and ridicule spread everywhere, in the nature of the day. But he felt it singly upon himself. The eyes of five young men next to him were on him, stinging, with no pretense of looking toward the parade. When he stared a direct challenge to them they looked away, blew cigarette smoke, began to sing *"Ciao, ciao, bambina,"* rocking their heads, laughing out the syllables. But their eyes never really left him. When he turned, they were back upon him, with dark mockery, stinging, as a cloud of flies sting at the wound in an animal, start away into a buzzing hover, then descend again.

Sarah was staring straight ahead. Her face seemed drained.

There was amusement in Salvatore's eyes, and Howard caught it.

Pietro took the measure of things, said the good floats were hours away, suggested a withdrawal to someplace quiet for coffee. He began to fight his way off with Howard and Sarah in tow, pointedly leaving all the others. Tarantella music bounced down to them between the houses. Their group cheered, behind them. Salvatore barreled down after Pietro's convoy. "Stay, stay!" he called. "Just for a minute! It's our Polifemo. You must see him with us. Then we'll have coffee together, we'll rest, we'll talk." His eyes filled with honest pleading.

Francesca was in his wake. "Turridu! Turridu!" She came up to them with a half-smile and a parcel wrapped in white cloth napkins. "Your mother says, how can you forget to give this to your friends? After you gave her no peace for two days?"

"Yes, yes, yes!" he said. "Here, from us. The best in the world! Now you will stay."

With eagerness trembling through his stained fingers, Salvatore pulled away the cloth to show the layers of dark and translucent honey crystal studded with almonds. In the streaming sun it could have been ambrosia, essence of the countryside's antique blessings.

While the others admired, Francesca turned back, to see Polifemo. But first she had glanced over her shoulder to catch Howard's eye, and to him alone, slyly and unmistakably, she made the sign of the horns. Two fingers spread; and half a smile.

Around the gift, three pairs of eyes were looking up to Howard with different styles of appeal.

Salvatore held the *torrone* out to him. "Try it. Please. It's a simple thing, but the best token of our hospitality."

Howard's hand swept down and the candy crashed to the street. "Your hospitality!"

His face was gripped in an astounding sneer. Gone, all blond clarity.

Some boys ran over, delight and neutrality on their faces; maybe something loud would happen.

From Salvatore came the rhetoric of hatred. "Our hospitality does not please you, signor Americano?"

Before fury could pour out, Sarah cried, "This is unbelievable! Why doesn't somebody say a sane word? For Christ's sake, Howard, apologize! What crazy scene are you trying to act out?"

He did not recognize her existence. But Pietro was also saying, "Shut up, Turridu! Owda didn't mean it that way. Did you, Owda?" He tried to grab both their arms, looking with all yearning into Howard's face. Which was a face of stone.

Eyes brimming, Pietro bent to try picking the cracked sweet out of the dust, where it had begun to draw flies.

But Salvatore kicked it out into the middle of the street. A policeman walking by crunched it against the stone.

He glanced at Salvatore's group, and so did the men with him.

Pietro was still crouched over a few honey splinters, looking up apologetically at everyone. Sarah's head had wilted. Howard stood fixed, his eyes open but unseeing, the pupils blank. Salvatore walked to him and whispered into his chest, "You and I had better step away from the others." Howard nodded, and strode off into the alleyway from which they had debouched before. Salvatore followed.

The tarantella music swirled down from the parade. Salvatore's mama emerged from it, with her bright red shawl, to learn how the Americans had liked her confection. Her son called back to her that she should wait; they would return in a minute. She should talk to the others. She obeyed.

Salvatore quickened his short steps and found the American in the little square where they had watched the float in rehearsal. Now the place was quite deserted, in favor of the parades. Only the American stood against the low wall, his head illumined, the swell of land framed below and beyond him. He was staring into the distance. There was the gloss of the sea and the temples in miniature along their ridge.

He turned his high face back, full of doubt, almost quizzical. "Well, what do you want to do?"

The Sicilian's face was tight. "I tell you what *you're* going to do. You're going to apologize. You'll do it, on your knees!"

Howard laughed.

"You offended my family, all of us. In public! Signor Americano, you beg for my pardon, and perhaps I'll forget it. We are not to be insulted! Not by foreigners! Not by you! Not by anyone!" The Sicilian prodded at his chest with thick third finger, harder each time, making dogged jabs of pain.

With another laugh, Howard pushed him a bit, for breathing space. The squat Sicilian didn't budge. Howard gave a quick two-armed thrust, hooking a leg behind. The pale-eyed face snapped back, dashed downward into the dust.

Then the American started after him, his hands not in fists, but open, wide, as if he wanted to explain.

But Salvatore came out of the dust with a wild oath and his knife catching a flare of sun.

A blast of rage ripped open the American's face. He seemed to make a towering run to the right but then lunged from the left side with his whole body, clipped the short man off his feet.

There was a flash of time when the Sicilian might have stabbed at the American's back, in midair. But he did not stab.

It was a clear case of clipping. Salvatore went down in agony; his knife clattered to the cobblestones. He tried to kick at the American's face, grip the knife, struggle to his feet, all at once. But when he was halfway up, Howard hit him with a flying tackle. The American was seventy pounds heavier and outrage roared as a beast in him. He flung his enemy against the top of the stone wall, where bones cracked against stone, and Salvatore fell, finally slashing in despair with his blade and bouncing off the rock, over the wall, into space. Rough rocks and dagger cacti waited, a hundred feet below.

Howard stood by the wall, dazed in the sun, his sweater arm torn, blood streaming along the tear.

Pietro and the women had come running just as the body bounced off the wall into the bright void. *"Hanno ammazzato Too-rreee-doo!"* they screamed.

"They've killed Turridu! They've killed Turridu!"

II

Five Stories

II

Familiar Usage in Leningrad

Not until he saw the silver swept-back jet with "Aeroflot" printed along its length in clean Cyrillic letters did Jeremy Pearl believe that he was really going to be free of Moscow. Two days of blessed relief. He mingled with the crowd at the boarding gate, under the morning sun, as cheerful and inconspicuous and perspiring as anyone there. The loudspeaker resounded pleasantly in his ears — the first pleasant loudspeaker he had heard in a month — calling flights to Kiev, Tpilisi, Tashkent, and finally his own, to Leningrad. Holiday mood swelled within him now, and gratitude toward the winged cylinder that was to lift him away. Really, these jets were splendid achievements.

Achievements: he winced at the word. After a month in Moscow, Jeremy had had more than enough of achievements, whether Ours or Theirs. A guide in the architecture section of the American Exhibition, he was weary of hearing his own voice praising the new glass skyscrapers along Park Avenue and weary of hearing the loudspeakers in Moscow grunting the latest news of pig iron tonnage from the Donbas. Driving out to the airport that morning, he had even been afraid to comment on the towering sunrise for fear that the taxi driver would start praising it as an achievement; socialist, capitalist, empyrean — what difference did it make? So he had not begun a conversation, which was a pity, because he hadn't yet met a Moscow cabby who lacked his malicious bit of gossip about Khrush-chev, the upper set, or the black market. Without a word, the two of them had rattled past the miles of yellowish block housing and the summer fields, in a brown car curi-ously like a Chevrolet of the late 1940s. But now, wedged into the lively crowd boarding the plane, he insisted, most firmly, to himself: No, a jet is *not* an achievement, nor a symbol, nor a statistic. It is a thing, handsome and ingen-ious, designed for human needs. People — Russians — grew cheerful at the prospect of flying in one. He, too, would be cheerful.

As he strapped on his safety belt, he listened with pleas-ure to the two young officers across the aisle arguing about the exact number of minutes the flight would take until the first touch on Leningrad runway. They settled on a bet payable in vodka, and the nearer leaned over toward Jer-emy to request his services as official timer. They seemed to have no immediate sense of his being a foreigner; this pleased him, and the long college weekends spent memo-rizing Russian verbs passed through his mind in grim but satisfying review. He looked at his watch, saying, "Do you think I'll have time to look at this again before we land?"

The nearer officer grinned in a self-congratulatory way all too familiar to Jeremy and said, "TU-104." He had a metal tooth.

"TU-104," Jeremy agreed.

TU-104. He thought of all those Russians at the Ex-hibition asking him with a child's good-natured intensity how long Nixon's flight to Moscow had taken and announc-ing that "our Kozlov" had flown from New York in "our TU-104" in eleven and a half hours. Then those metal-toothed grins, mixed with mock compassion, as if Nixon had obviously crawled all the way on his hands and knees, when

Jeremy admitted to not knowing how many hours the American jet had taken. TU-104. Did the hundredth and thousandth person to ask an identical question really have a sense that the question still existed? Faces seemed to say so, crowding in upon him, eager or doubtful or hostile, workers' or students' or agitators' faces, faces from Sverdlovsk and Kharkov and Tomsk, lined or blunt or not recently shaved, too many faces, for thirty-two days. It was not only his having worked too long in Moscow's suspicious air, pressed into its bulbous chaos, that had tired Jeremy. It was being plunged into Mass Questions for the first time. He had been a bookish young man, and now he was battered every day by eight or ten hours of bragging and apologizing and arguing. On the second day he had remembered that these pouring crowds were composed of Russian people; by the fourth he could perceive only Soviet population units, endlessly repeating themselves, except for a very few, and all wanting to talk with heat about We and They.

Who cared, finally? At this heretical thought he glanced around guiltily — a new habit. The officers had stopped consulting the altimeter set like a clock into the cabin's wall up front, because they were fascinated by Jeremy's loafers. Soon they would want to talk, to be hospitable and jolly, to compare the number of cubic meters in their respective university dormitories — Moscow versus Harvard — to chat about all the things Jeremy once had thought he had come to the Soviet Union to hear. It would be decent, honest We and They talk, urgent with peace and friendship until certain taboo words came up: governments, missiles, Hungary, Guatemala. So he turned, guiltily, to the window and watched the last traces of the city below. Even the white mass of the university disappeared, the world's largest inhabited stone cake; and the Moscow River gave a last glint. The fields over which they were flying now were not checkered like those of Europe or Pennsylvania. They were broad and Russian and dull, fading away into vague forests.

He was glad to be leaving Moscow for a while, since he certainly wasn't the type to be exhibited to mobs. Look: a genuine, pudgy piece of Americana with thick glasses! He was tired of Russians barging up to him at the Exhibition, asking, "Who are you?" Or, rather, "What is your father?" What snobs these workers and peasants were! My father is an accountant, a man who keeps columns of figures for capitalists. Then the agitators' superior smiles, full of implication: You see, Comrades, you needn't discuss with this round young person; his family exploits the masses. Once, when an agitator had started the father routine with him, Jeremy had leaned over to a charming Russian girl in the crowd and whispered, "I'll tell you a secret. My father is a nervous Jewish Marxist."

"So is mine," the girl answered, and winked. Then she vanished across the hot black pavement, beyond the crowds, her blue print summer dress flying after her. It had been a relationship of typical length for Jeremy Pearl, considering that he had liked the girl and she was attractive. For an hour afterward, he had been too rattled to make his brilliant explanation of America's entry into Korea. Well, in thirty-two days and nights he had only succeeded in grazing a few lives, at best. And he was tired, furthermore, of the other American guides in their identical blue sweaters, all busy and young and admiring themselves in their roles of guides and taking notes. Shiny guide fish out of school water, flopping and gulping because there turned out to be so much conflict in the world. He congratulated himself on having severed connections from the jovial shoal that was also spending these two day of leave in Leningrad; he grinned to remember their faces when he had told them he was only going to the Hermitage anyway, to see some Lorenzo Lottos and Giorgione's bright-red *Judith*. Let them have something to talk about on the train.

The stewardess was at his arm, watching him mumble to himself. She asked again, *"Ne khotite fruktovoi vody?"* The ubiquitous gas water, in heavy glasses. Do you know, he asked the girl silently, that the Soviets have achieved the world's worst cherry soda? She jiggled the tray a little impatiently, but smiled at him. She had no makeup; she wore a simple white blouse; some wisps of her hair were rebellious. Who ever heard of a stewardess shaped like a dumpling? *"Spasibo,"* he said aloud, and took a glass.

As soon as the sweet gas water came out, so did the flies. They flew busy circles around the sun motes, buzzing and colliding as if the TU-104 were any Moscow restaurant. They dipped their hairy bodies into the gas water and tried to escape with their sugar bubbles before being swatted with rolled-up *Pravda*'s. A passenger called on God to curse the Aeroflot. Wonderful, thought Jeremy, socialist self-criticism in action. Then the cabin door opened and an oldish man stepped out, wearing work trousers and an undershirt. "Citizens," he said, "I want to explain about the flies." An angry murmur went up. "We apologize," the man said, brushing at his ear. "It is only during the hot months that we have this — inconvenience, but we fly such a full schedule with so many Comrades on vacation that there is no time to fumigate between flights. Of course, we do have fly swatter brigades — strong ladies," and the man's eye yielded a twinkle. "But they only get the flies unfit to survive. The clever ones all hide under the arms of the seats. Comrades, what can we do? It's nature. Thank you." He bowed and withdrew as the passengers clapped and hooted. The officers caught Jeremy's eye and did begin a conversation on We and They, insects and airlines, which Jeremy enjoyed. The jet landed before they knew it, lowering past bogs and stunted fir trees, and he shook hands, exchanging wishes of peace and friendship for the ten thousandth time that summer. All three had forgotten the bet when they separated, relaxed and benign, into the midmorning. Jeremy was in an excellent mood for his visit to the Hermitage.

But he did not see the Hermitage that day. Soviet red tape wound around and around his singleness, forcing him to debate at every turn the Intourist assumption that because he was not a delegation, he did not exist. While groups from Iowa, Indonesia, and East Germany bustled by, he had ample time to study wall portraits of Lenin and Chinese dignitaries. Two hours to get a place in a limousine for the city; an hour and a half to find an overstuffed room at the Hotel Astoria; two hours to win a place at table in the hotel dining room and have cold salmon, tomato salad, and *blinchiki* brought to him.

It was after four o'clock when he finally stood out in the cooling air. Too late for the museums, he wandered through the great northern spaciousness of Leningrad's center, the planned streets and squares, the imitative but gracious pallaces, neoclassical, rococo, peeling now but still defying the marshy Finnish winds with strange pastel greens and yellows, with porticoes and rows of columns; surely never so many columns erected anywhere else so far from the Mediterranean. The city still rose out of the brimming

Neva waters like a mirage — "Peter's creation." Jeremy felt strangely at home. Beneath the cupola of the Isaac Cathedral and the admiralty building's golden needle glinting toward the oblique sun, he walked through a shadow into the European past, when the city's delegations had been Quarenghis and Rastrellis invited to design an architecture complete for their hosts. He let himself into the city of Peter and Catherine, of summer's white nights in Pushkin and Dostoevsky, of winter's three o'clock sunsets in Gogol. He refused to draw gray conclusions from the squalor pressing on all sides; if there was squalor side by side with dignity, let it be called picturesque, for he did not want to make decisions. It was New York and Peiping that required decisions: what have men wrought there? And, of course, Moscow, with its awful momentousness in the air, the ringing of the bell at the Kremlin gate to announce the silent blind limousines swooshing forth into the emptiness of Red Square. But in Leningrad, Peter's town, the momentousness had passed by. At least for a traveler.

He whistled softly as he strolled under a huge coffered archway into the square fronting the Winter Palace. The square was immense beyond belief, as if miles of marshland — half the frontier of Finland — had been drained and paved and bordered with a neat gardenlike set of palaces. The shaft of the Alexander monument stood stunted amid the whelming space. Toy Russian figures walked singly or in twos at drab intervals. Jeremy's imagination raced; he was standing in the unfillable Palace Square he had read about: "The first time there is a crowd in Petersburg, the city will be crushed . . . a crowd would mean a revolution." He stood alone, he and the Alexander column and the few toy figures, but in his mind the carriages rolled up to the green Winter Palace behind horses supple and glossy under the lanterns; the bejeweled and haughty — Speranskis and Karenins and Volkonskis — poured out, dwarfed by the immensities. And tiny Trotsky mastering the raging square with words.

A sudden wind swept across from the Neva. He put his hands deep into his pockets and slouched off across the square, now bleak as a tundra. He had almost reached the archway again and was beginning to wonder what to do next when he found a crisply folded paper in his right pocket. It was obviously not a ruble note, because all his rubles came in wads or sheaves. He put on his horn-rimmed glasses and held the paper close to his eyes in the dimming light. "To Elizaveta" was written in a cursory American hand. Elizaveta? Yes, the note from that tall boy, Bob What's-his-name, who had come to the exhibition from the Vienna Youth Conference via the north. "Met this great girl in Leningrad, you see? Speaks English like a dream. Want her to drop down here before I go to Tashkent. Listen, get this note to her when you're up there, will you, Jerry? Be a friend. She may introduce you to some interesting people; you could use some —" Thinking of Bob What's-his-name, Jeremy started to crumple the note and look for a sewer. But he reconsidered. The girl's address was on the Nevsky Prospect, quite far from the river. He could take a slow twilight stroll along the Nevsky and talk to Gogol. With luck, the address would be hard to find, so that his evening would be almost accounted for. Then, back to the hotel: caviar, hot tea with extra sugar, and to bed. Tomorrow, the Hermitage all day.

"Just step out onto the Nesky, and it already smells of strolling," said Gogol to Jeremy. "True, true," he answered. The Prospect was still wide, lively, and clean, at least as far as he could tell in the dusk. Strollers there were: the men in sandals and bell-bottomed trousers, women in neat jackets over print dresses, children in sailors' outfits. Behind him, the admiralty spire had just lost its high tip of sunlight, while in the government cheese and wine shops the lights were coming on, splashing the patient queues. People were arm in arm, and Jeremy was with Gogol.

By the time he found the address, the Prospect had peacefully deteriorated. Elizaveta's building had five stories, poor and damp-looking, in a neighborhood that seemed still to be quivering from the Nazi siege. Jeremy turned into an open entranceway leading to a series of murky inner courtyards. He decided not to ask anyone for directions to the right staircase, because he had no idea of the mood of the Leningrad authorities toward Americans paying calls. Bob What's-his-name, who didn't speak a word of Russian, must have visited the house. But, still — Jeremy stumbled awhile in suffocating darkness. The shutters on the inner courtyard were all pulled, although it was still August. Pallid electric bulbs burned in the entryways; someone was practicing a Rachmaninoff prelude on an inadequate piano. Finally he climbed a dark staircase, toward the fourth floor. The wrought-iron railing wobbled in his hand. Doors along the way, two to a landing, were incredibly decrepit, with some unheard-of kind of stuffing falling out of them as if they were old quilts. The place was impregnated with a sour smell, a mingling of cabbage, sweat, bad plaster, and nineteenth-century rainfalls. Past and present blurred in Jeremy's mind again. Gogol, quite uninvited, warned him that if they were frying fish in the kitchen, there would probably be so much smoke that he wouldn't even be able to see the cockroaches. "Take your big nose and go away," Jeremy said. He knocked on the door, much too loudly.

After a moment, the door opened one third, and a crumpled old face looked up at him. Another old lady, less crumpled than the first, stood in the background. "*Dobryi vecher*," he said, trying to greet both of them. "I'd like to speak to Elizaveta if I may." They shuffled away, leaving the door as it was, and he heard one of them saying, "A cultured young man . . ." Jeremy could see an icon of the Virgin and an upholstered couch shaped like a donkey's back. Then a slender girl stood in his line of sight — rather tall, with an unfinished thought on her face and a curl to the corners of her eyes and mouth that gave her a smile even if she wasn't smiling. As she was not now. She wore the usual Russian print dress; her summer-brown hair was braided. In one hand she had a folder of papers and a pencil imprisoned by her thumb. She waited, neutrally. "Yes," she said, "what is it, Comrade?"

"I'm sorry to trouble you when you are working," Jeremy said, "but here is a note for you, from an American named Bob — " She grabbed not the note but Jeremy's wrist, and pulled him inside, slamming the door.

"Are you an American?" she whispered, in English, looking at his face and then at his loafers.

"Yes, I am. I work at the Exhibition in Moscow."

"Then don't you know you should not have come here? It is very dangerous. Has anyone seen you? Oh God, that stupid — " Elizaveta still seemed to be smiling because of the strange curve to her face.

"No one saw me," he said. "I'm sorry, I didn't think —"

"Speak Russian," Elizaveta snapped. "Those old witches will have a fit." The two ladies were sewing in a corner by the same lamp, with the inevitable fringed orange shade.

One room for all: there was a bed in another corner, probably Elizaveta's, because a lamp-lit writing desk was next to it, and a small glass-enclosed bookcase with standard Russian authors. A cot was made up near the couch, and a wooden table with a bowl of cucumbers stood in the middle of the room. A second golden icon, of Saint George, and a print of old Petersburg hung on the walls. Jeremy started to explain, in Russian, that Bob had given him no information at all about the Leningrad situation, but the more crumpled lady crept up, pulling her black shawl close, and said, "It is time for *him* to go." Jeremy edged toward the door.

"But maybe *he* is not ready to go," Elizaveta said angrily, taking hold of his sleeve.

"Liza," the old lady croaked, "your foreign friends are going to ruin us. Especially if they are so idiotic — "

"He's not my friend, and it's not his fault. He just arrived from Moscow and knows nothing about — "

"It's time for him to go!" said the other lady. She was frantic. "To *go!*"

Jeremy stood, miserably. Elizaveta was still holding his sleeve. She looked at him with quick sympathy. "This is terrible for you. You were only trying to do a favor."

"To *go!* To *go!*" wailed the second lady from her corner, as the first crossed herself, mumbling.

"Oh, shut up!" Elizaveta said. She threw on a brown cloth coat, took Jeremy's arm, and steered him onto the stairs. "Let's go for a walk, Kolya," she said loudly, as if to an audience on the stairs. "Toward your brother's."

The door slammed behind them. She propelled him out through the courtyards and onto the night-filled Nevsky without letting him say a word. He was still burning with embarrassment when they had joined the strollers going back toward the river.

"Please forgive me," he stammered. "I certainly didn't mean — It was the last thing —"

"Don't mind the old ladies. The less they have to live for, the more they worry about it."

She was not looking at him. He considered saying, "I apologize. Deeply. Good-by," but she still had an automatic hold on his arm. "Who are they?" he asked instead.

"Who are who? Oh, them. My grandmother and her friend. I think the friend is *her* grandmother, but they're ashamed of it. We all love each other madly."

"I don't see very well in the dark," Jeremy said. "Do you mind telling me whether you are smiling or not?"

"Perhaps. I remain, however, inscrutable."

True. He had no idea whether or not her anger was still near the surface.

"My name is Jeremy," he said. "You know, something like the prophet." He had pronounced it in English.

"Of course, Ieremia. My grandmother knows all the prophets by heart, which accounts for the wisdom of her approach to life. I am so furious at her, and you, and Bob."

A block of silence. Jeremy said, "What do you do?"

"I am a translator. Which reminds me. You know, Ieremia, that you speak a very clean, exact Russian. If I were not so mortified over this evening, we could perfect it. Why did you learn Russian so well?"

"I like it."

"Are you a spy?"

"Yes." This time Jeremy knew that she was smiling, because they passed under a street lamp — three high bright globes in the pawnbroker's pattern — and her teeth flashed a little. Suddenly she pushed him into a doorway and said, "Well, let me show you how to be a good spy. First, take off that stupid tie. Come on." It was his regular striped traveling tie. But he took it off. "Now open your top button and put out your shirt collar — wide, like this — over your jacket. Good. Now off with those glasses. Too American. Lean toward me when I take your arm, put a smug expression on your face — excellent — and we have an ambitious young Soviet engineer out with his solemn translator friend. Perfect couple."

They walked a while more, into the old Petersburg section, across the Griboyedov Canal and past the former Kazan Cathedral, now an antireligious museum. He was afraid to ask questions that would show how little he knew of the city. He cleared his throat as if in preparation for an important remark. "The streets of Leningrad," he said, "are very clean."

"Of course they are," she said. "We have a program of compulsory-voluntary immaculateness."

"You mean one can't even have dirt if one wants to? One's own small pile of dirt?"

"Really, you bourgeoisie have such decadent ideas."

"But I represent the Western democracies," said Jeremy. "I am shocked that you Russians cannot have freedom of dirt."

"Citizen Little Man, we have greater goals in mind. Your obsolete private dirt will have to go. You may share all the rich collective dirt you want at the *kolhoz.*"

"You know," Jeremy said, "this being a Little Man is not comfortable. They chased me down these very streets with bronze hoofs. They stole my greatcoat after I went without tea to save for it. Now they take away my pile of dirt. What a life."

"Ah, Little Man, I sympathize. They took away your czar."

"They took away my nobility," he said.

"They took away your room."

"They took away my family."

"And now they want your dirt," said Elizaveta.

"And now they want my dirt. After midnight I come out alone on the Nevsky and drop cigarette butts in my favorite gutters. But in the morning — "

"Nothing?"

"Nothing."

"A socialist triumph."

"Communist repression. One night I left old copies of *Izvestia* everywhere."

"Vicious capitalist espionage!"

"Courageous democratic action. But what's the use?"

"None," said Elizaveta. "Any other questions? Feel free to ask questions. The people must be educated."

"That's true. You must catch up to and overtake America."

"But *you* must meet the Soviet challenge, economically, militarily — "

"Who knows?" Jeremy said.

"Who knows?" agreed Elizaveta.

They had reached the river. In the glisten of the fast water, lights from eighteenth-century windows threatened to move downstream but held their own, at the last minute, against the current. Jeremy put on his glasses. He and Elizaveta laughed, in great relief, delighted with each other.

There were few cars along the embankment. Elizaveta's face was in the darkness, but her eyes, like the river, caught little points of reflected light. Jeremy imagined that he could still see the unfinished thought on her face and could feel in her slenderness the pathos of all the slim girls and admirable ladies who filled his memory from the pages of Turgenev and Tolstoy. A wave of feeling surprised him, a *frisson* down through his ankles: he felt that he was shaken in a confusion as to who or where he was, where the pages of his imagination ended and where he had actually begun to stand in the night above the River Neva with this girl close to him.

Elizaveta extended a slim finger and touched Jeremy's right cheek. "Little Person," she said. She began to trace patterns along his cheekbone and the soft center below it.

"I see that you understand very well who I am," he said. He took off his glasses again and shoved them into his jacket pocket. Elizaveta's finger continued to drift across his face. The night became a blur. He reached his hand through the night toward the place where he remembered her face to be, saying, "But you are an Aleksandra or a Natasha."

"No," she said, "no!" and she pressed his palm full against her face. "I'm a Little Person too, the least in the world." He could feel her face moving against his palm as she spoke. "Only the Little Persons are still alive." He moved closer to her and heard her words as whispers of breath against his ear. "Ieremi"— she had softened the name —"the others are all dead. They want us to be dead with them. They don't want us to feel what it is to be alive."

Suddenly he felt her lips on his, with a terrible hunger. They kissed again and again and held to each other, afraid to let go; he felt her hands pressing at his temples. Before they parted, the glistening Neva waters that had passed them at the beginning had long since flowed into the Gulf of Finland. Passers-by, ever fewer, smiled at them. The two leaned against the stone parapet, watching the swift wide

waters that came newly on, and they hardly knew where
to begin finding words again. Time was short between
them. They had no place to go, Jeremy thought; it was
already late. Tomorrow was the important word in their
lives. "Tomorrow," he said, just as Elizaveta hesitantly
asked, "What are you going to do tomorrow?"

She had instructed him in the art of meeting invisibly
during daylight. He was to find her in the morning crowd
near the antireligious museum — there was always a crowd
near the antireligious museum, which had a jolly waxworks
exhibition of bad priests and obscurantists — and then he
was to pass through her field of vision, walking slowly. She
would follow him down the Nevsky at a gradually decreas-
ing distance until they were side by side. "Fading together,"
she called it; a way of meeting "questionable human beings"
without there having been a place where so-and-so was seen
greeting so-and-so. That night, as he fell asleep, Jeremy
wondered, a little petulantly, why he hadn't learned this
before, until he realized that she would be the first Russian
he was going to meet privately in daytime.

In his room at the Astoria, he awoke to sunlight on the
ornate mirror with another start of confusion as to where
and who. He put on his glasses. The room was Russified
Victorian. Gilt, fringed cushions, angels carved from heavy
wood, furniture resting on thumping big lions' feet. He
hadn't even learned her last name. In fact, he couldn't
remember what she looked like. There was a sense of her
cleanliness and slenderness in the dusk, her words and
touch; delicious, but he would never recognize her in a
crowd. It was over. Typical, typical, Jeremy muttered as
he pulled on his clothes.

He ran in terror from the beaming fat waitress who

wanted him to sit down for three hours over tea in a glass and fried eggs. In the square he bought two sweet rolls from a girl in a white smock at a pushcart, and he half trotted, munching, toward the meeting place. The Nevsky Prospect was streaming with people on their way to office work, looking almost as wilted as their old briefcases. The sun was hot. Jeremy arrived at the semicircular colonnade of the former Kazan Cathedral a half-hour early, and he was just about to find twenty reasons why it was so unfortunate an imitation of St. Peter's when he saw her. She was unmistakable, as slim and fresh as he remembered, with her light-brown hair brushed back, a touch of lipstick. She was wearing a neat sweater buttoned up the front and even a string of glass beads. She looked through him as if he were one of the wax statues inside. Oh, yes, of course; Jeremy remembered and walked obediently away toward the looming yellow admiralty building.

In a moment he felt an arm slip into his and he smelled lavender soap. She laughed into his ear. "Good morning, *gospodin* spy. What's the password?"

Jeremy said, "No answer, Elizabeth," which makes a foolish rhyme in Russian, no better than "See you later, alligator." But she seemed satisfied. Now that it was true that he was going to spend the day with a marvelous Russian girl, he decided not to waste it. Daytime: sociological information; evening: love. Accordingly, he began his interrogation. "I don't even know your last name," he said.

"I don't have one," she answered. "Or, rather, I did have one until the Revolution, but they took it away. They renamed me Steelworks. Steelworks in the name of Kirov. But you can call me just Liza." She used *ty* — "thee" — with him, which threw Jeremy even more off balance, since he had learned all his conversational Russian in the polite

form. He stumbled twice, trying to begin a sentence. Elizaveta laughed again. "You're pretending to have trouble so
that we'll have to speak English. Well, we won't. It's too
inconvenient, and too — cold."

They never got to the Hermitage. Lorenzo Lotto, Elizaveta said laughing, Jeremy would always have with him;
for her, he had only one day. She wanted to go where they
could "talk all the time and chase each other and run in
the sun."

They were in a taxi, driving through scanty landscape
toward Peterhof. The Gulf of Finland, seeming frigid and
forlorn even in August, lay to their right, with Kronstadt's
bristle of cranes in the distance. To the left, the birch-
scattered flatness never blessed by nature and too recently
blasted by the siege. Charred hulks of the old estate houses
stood on slight rises of the ground. Jeremy would have
asked the cab driver for his memories of the war if Elizaveta
had not assumed a Ukrainian accent, pronouncing all her
g's like *h*'s, and told the driver they were both summer
vacationers in town for two days. She also introduced
Jeremy as a young Party official from Albania who really
knew Russian quite well. The driver pretended great interest in Albania, so Jeremy gave a report on conditions
there, stressing agricultural problems and Muslim reaction,
while Elizaveta ran her finger up and down his back. After
the driver had thanked Jeremy for the tip, he pointed good-
naturedly. "You're not from Albania, Comrade, and she is
not Ukrainian."

"Quite right," Jeremy said. "I'm American." This sent the
driver into gales of laughter.

He said, "And she, I suppose, is also American, from
Hollywood [*Golivud*]. And I'm from Hawaii [*Gavai*]. Very

warm in *Gavai*." He was still muttering happily to himself about Hawaii as he drove off.

The two spent their bright hours in the park at Peterhof under the high gross majesty of the palace on its hill — the only hill within miles — with the splash of all its fountains and the blue marine canal gathering their waters to flow into the sea, that northern finger of sea for which eighteenth-century czars were so grateful. Elizaveta described the rubble left by the siege, and pointed with pride to the restorations, complete even to Tritons and Venuses descending in a brilliant gilded cascade. Suddenly she said to Jeremy, "You don't like them, do you?"

"Well —" he said. The restorations were too garish; the glittering yellow sculpture reminded him of golf trophies.

"You realize, my dear boy, what the people went through here and what it means to have this place as theirs again?"

Jeremy looked worried. He was afraid he would start spouting about art and society. "Poor Jeremy," Elizaveta said, touching his chin. Her mood had changed again. "I'm not going to make you argue. This is a day for Little Persons."

And it was. They ran through the parks. They splashed in every fountain capable of being splashed in, bought ice cream from saintly ladies in white, and then they were shivering together at the prow of the excursion boat back to Leningrad across the cold gray wash of the gulf. The city was a long blur ahead of them, except where the golden needle of the Petropavlovsk fortress caught a late gleam of sun and cauterized the dimness.

It was the edge of night when they were in front of the stolid Astoria Hotel, certainly not to say good-by, but not knowing where to go. Jeremy was saying, "Elizaveta, come

up to my room. It's quiet and private. You'll love it; it has
a lamp with an orange fringed shade and a picture of a
nice peasant girl gathering something — radishes, I think
— that makes her very happy."

"Oh, Ieremi, I want to very much. More than you want
me to, I think. But it's impossible."

"Don't radishes make you happy?"

Elizaveta smiled, perhaps. "Very. And so do you. But if
they find me in a foreigner's room at the Astoria, I'm
through. I have a bad name already." He raised his eyebrows, but she said, "No, we have no time to go into that.
Anyway, our public crimes are personal matters. Don't
meddle. I haven't asked you how you treat Negroes."

"I promise to salute every Negro I meet if you will come
to my room."

"Ieremi, it would be horrible for you, too. Tass would
give it bigger propaganda right now than a new Sputnik.
How they would love to find an American lecher spreading
his poisons around the Soviet masses. I would have to testify
that you lured me with visions of Wall Street. What would
your mother think?"

"You're playing with me, aren't you?"

"Playing with you? Do you have any idea what this game
may cost? Do you really think — Oh, never mind. Next
thing, you will accuse me of self-pity, then flightiness. Go
ahead. I'll give you ten minutes for the whole list."

"I'm sorry," he said. "I always seem to be sorry. I suppose
I wanted to be serious for a moment."

"For seriousness we definitely have no time, sweet friend."
Elizaveta took his hand in both of hers and pulled him toward the hotel entrance. "Come on," she said, "we can have
some wine and we can dance upstairs in the ballroom. Excellent cure for seriousness."

"But won't that be just as — inconvenient? For you?"

"No, no. It's so crowded and obvious that they will never notice us. Just don't forget to be one half the perfect Soviet couple. Smug expression. And let me speak most of the time — which I would probably do anyway."

While they were riding up in the elevator, Elizaveta whispered, "What Russian word can you pronounce most easily?"

"Radishes," Jeremy whispered.

"Good. If anyone official wants to talk to you, just say, 'radishes.' "

The Astoria ballroom. High ceiling, shiny waxed floor, small round tables packed in as tightly as salmon eggs, palm fronds hanging helplessly, corks popping from mediocre Georgian wine, an eight-piece band, Guy Lombardo style, pot-shaped middle-class couples pushing each other anxiously back and forth to a series of variations on "Moscow Evenings."

"Lord," Jeremy whispered. "They're all from the Bronx."

The headwaiter seated them at a table with an imperturbably well-nourished, fortyish couple. He wore a dark suit and a wide tie with a pattern that looked like watermelons; she had a frilly white blouse and too much perfume. She was slicing a Kiev cutlet that oozed with butter, and he was toying with the fatty embroidery of his poached sturgeon. "They really don't know how to play dance music here," she was saying. "In Paris it's different. We've been to Paris," she said, turning to Elizaveta. And then to Jeremy, "Don't you think so?"

"Radishes," Jeremy said.

"Pardon?" said she.

But Elizaveta was already on her feet, saying, "You know,

Kolya, I don't think we have time for dinner after all. Your brother will be waiting."

They were out in the street, looking up at the tall baroque dome of the Isaac Cathedral. "God save us from the Astoria ballroom," said Jeremy. Elizaveta seemed thoughtful. "Do you know anything about the Bronx?" he asked.

"No, unless you mean those wild horses in your *kovboi* stories."

Jeremy locked Elizaveta in a tremendous bear hug. "Oh, absurd, absurd," he said, in English.

"I don't know exactly what you mean," said Elizaveta in Russian, "but it's true." She struggled to free her arms, and then put them around his neck.

They clung together. This time Jeremy felt desire run through him like summer lightning. He tried to kiss the corners of her lips, where the smiles were. Elizaveta whispered and began to touch his face with soft kisses. "Oh, I don't care," she said. "Come on. Pay another visit to my apartment. This time I invite you."

"But —"

She put her finger over his lips. "No one will notice. You look completely Russian now. I've ruined you."

The last hint of summer dusk hung on and on, as it does in the north. They leaned close, strolling down the wide Nevsky again. Finally he asked, "Will the grandmothers be out?"

"Of course not. They are much too old."

"But, couldn't they drop into the communal kitchen or something?" He heard his voice growing plaintive.

"No, no, no, they always eat early." Elizaveta laughed softly. "They won't mind us. They'll sit in the far corner

and turn their backs and bend over their sewing. They
have an incredible amount of sewing to do."

"But, still —"

"Oh, Ieremi, dear boy, it won't be embarrassing. We just
have to be a little quieter than you are used to being in the
Western democracies. Unless you can solve our housing
within ten minutes." They walked on in silence, past
the dark colonnade of the antireligious museum where they
had "faded together" in the morning. Elizaveta clung still
more closely to his arm. "You'll see, Ieremi. It won't be so
bad. We're all used to it."

"Well, I'm not." He tried to sound good-natured.

"But that's just the way it is."

"The way it *is?*" he asked, in desolation. "Is that the way
it was with Bob What's-his-name and every other What's-
his-name?"

She stopped dead. "What do you *want* of this world?"
she asked, coldly. "I suppose you think you've said something cruel. It's worse than that; it's stupid. Sometimes I
think you Americans *are* corrupt. You always must *own*
things. That's the only relationship you can understand."
She turned away from him.

Oh, God, thought Jeremy, here it is, the inevitable.

But Elizaveta led him instead to a street lamp, and she
took his worried face in her hands. "Ieremi," she said,
"timid boy, accept what I am offering. Love is the one
thing here that is not complicated. Perhaps with you it is
just the opposite, but now you are *chez nous* and you must
do as we do. Agreed?" His throat would not let him say the
word. "Agreed?" asked Elizaveta.

"Yes, agreed," he said.

They walked along through the murk-filled inner court-
yards, up the cabbaged stairway with its doors waning in

decrepitude, Jeremy playing silent word games to ease his embarrassment: I'm always inhibited when the room is inhabited. He admired the slope of Elizaveta's slim back as she put the key into the lock, without making a sound, and then they were in the modest room with its golden Saint George and the Virgin, and sway-backed couches, sets of Tolstoy and Chekhov, orange fringed lamps, and the one solid table with its bowl of cucumbers. Both the old ladies shook hands with Jeremy, addressing him as "young man." The more crumpled asked him whether he would like a cucumber, and the other began to suggest, somewhat indirectly, that since he was a foreigner it was getting to be time for him to go. But when they saw that Elizaveta was stretching a brown blanket like a curtain in front of her bed, suspending it from the book cabinet and a clothing rack, reaching up on tiptoe with her arms upraised, the two ladies smiled and nodded and patted Jeremy's arm. Then they bundled off toward their sewing corner. Russian women. Elizaveta accepted him quietly into the deep shadows she had created, where love is the one thing not complicated.

They were walking, hand in hand, down the gloom of the Nevsky's tag end, toward the Moscow Station. It was late in the evening. The Red Arrow was leaving Leningrad in half an hour, and Jeremy had to be on it in order to stand at his post when the Exhibition floodgates opened at eleven the next morning. Empty buses ground by. "I haven't even asked you about your family," he said.

"Don't. We are Russians. When we aren't busy killing each other, someone rolls in the artillery from Europe. Only my brother and I were left after the siege. He went out to grow corn in Siberia. And I stayed on."

"Why?"

"Oh, I still love poor Leningrad. I hold the grand-mothers' hands, and go to concerts, and wait for people like you." Elizaveta leaned fondly against his arm for a moment. Then she said, "Ieremi, the station is no place for a Russian to be with a foreigner either. We shall have to fade apart."

"*Nu ladno.* Well" — he hesitated — "all right. But when can we meet again?"

She shook her head. "Ieremi, I'm in trouble as it is."

He tried to slow the pace of their walk. He closed his eyes and leaned more heavily toward Elizaveta. He began to hum. Then he said, "I suppose you admire all your Russian *Romeo and Juliet* music — Prokofiev, Tchaikov-sky."

She laughed, too quietly. "You're not very subtle, you know. I suppose I like Prokofiev, somewhat. But I love Mozart, like you. Did you forget already, stupid boy?" He opened his eyes. They were in a blurred square with a monument, and the Moscow Station bulked ahead.

"Liza," he said, "where will we be after we fade apart? Tell me."

"I don't know. I don't know, my friend. Where we were before, it seems. Nowhere."

"You just don't understand!" he burst out. "Maybe you can be brave like a Turgenev woman, and maybe you think life is fine with me because our police don't follow me at night. Maybe you think a moment's love is the solution for everything."

"Please, Ieremi! Please, please! We've had something. Isn't that more than nothing? Who are we to — " She could not go on. She burst into wild tears, amazing him, and kissed his face. Then she was gone, running, while he still

leaned toward the place where she had been, as a stalk
leans after the wind.

Steam rose in clouds past the windows: a samovar in the
train buffet was softly brewing. Through the station a
loudspeaker echoed, announcing the departure of the Red
Arrow for Moscow. Its voice bulged with the tedious Soviet assumption that the departure of every train will be wel-
comed by history.

A Friendly Cycle

WE cycled in one day the ninety or so miles from Stratford to Cambridge. It was a fine June day, with a gentle breeze blowing behind us from west to east across the flattish center of the island. The only hills we faced, early in the day, were modest. I reveled in strength, in the flow of air past my face and the easy slopes with their grotesque fruit trees. I was a much stronger cyclist than he. I would ride far ahead, imagining myself as a dwindling figure while he huffed in anger, and I would agonizingly prolong and prolong the moment of slowing down. Sometimes I would slow down enough for him to catch up, say, half the distance between us, when I would put on another burst of speed, nonchalantly, of course, showing neither strain nor recognition of his approach and retreat. Again I would dwindle, rejoicing in the freedom I could win so easily from his supervisory personality, speeding out in grand privacy along the road. Because my legs happened to be so much stronger (the outcome of years of jumping for basketballs while he had been doing sedentary, useful things), I could control this part of our relationship easily, and, admittedly, cruelly. We rested when I wanted to rest, which wasn't often. How could he, the more tired one, ever choose to stop? I was far ahead but, in agreement with the tacit assumptions of bicycling and goodness of character, not aware of the fact — just rolling along, enjoying the countryside. How satisfying it was for once not to be forcibly dawdling behind, at his mulish pace, watching him spoil every interesting house and vista by waving his committee chairman's hand at them. Free of his unction and his slowness, I could glide through the world stopping only when the spirit moved me. If he stopped, I would be five miles away before I chose to notice — after all, we were there for impersonal aims of growth and education and, we agreed, could hardly be expected to watch out constantly for each other — which meant that he would have to struggle on, humiliated, for half an hour until he found me, refreshed by the rest he had chosen, patiently sitting by the side of the road reading my paperback Keats. Needless to say, I would be tactful as could be, never referring to his slowness, but asking with devastating innocence whether anything had gone wrong with the bike. He would have to lie (which he did not) or admit that he had taken a moment's rest to look over a certain cottage or churchyard more carefully, whereupon I would say, "Good. Then we can push on." And I would hop on the seat to go tearing off again. But he, of course, was still panting from his effort to minimize the rest he knew I had already taken, which rest I had maximized by exerting myself beforehand to the most heroic speeds, since I knew that *he* had stopped somewhere behind. Complicated, but enough to inspire me to peak performance. His effort to save face would always be costly; I doubled his agonies by my fresh start, reinforced physically by relaxation and morally by knowing that he, after all, had chosen to rest first and we did have a noble collective goal for the day's cycling. So we really rested when I wanted to, and I would be renewed enough by the time he caught up to me. He would have to plead, panting, that we stay a little longer. Again, I would be tactful. This was all part of my revenge for his moral superiority.

In college that spring he had been able to finish all the arduous and worthy committee tasks that I had been too weak to carry through. In return, he had, of course, exacted from me the tribute of abject Christian humility, such as he claimed to have achieved already. At our age (freshmen in college) all the vistiges of religious attitude were of crucial importance. Humility before the universe and other men was an imperative. I groveled and groveled before him, but I could never bow low enough. He sat in his splendid pride, urging me to emulate the humility through which he was enabled to do the tedious chores before us (washing the feet of Christ), and I, in fierce bursts of ambition, would swear that no one could possibly reach the levels of humility I had in mind. I had been foolish enough to stammer out to him my notions of a personal God, to which he replied with a set speech about his own concern with "the divine." I should have known that he was false on this issue, which he used against me very effectively, but I was too torn with guilt to evaluate other men. Such was the emotional dynamite of that age, not to explode finally until our summer abroad.

During our month in good, green England we had obviously begun to build toward our explosion, and we both knew it. About a week before our epic cycle (epicycle, I called it — but he didn't laugh) from Stratford to Cambridge, we were staying in a sweet Channel village in southern Dorset called something like Nonnydale. He and I had shared the travelers' intimacies. We planned and ate together, we washed our Dacron underwear together in basins, and we knew each other's smells quite well. For a few weeks we had even shared large, clean double beds in an innocent way as part of the Cyclist Touring Club's routine of hosteling in private homes.

But in the Nonnydale night I was awakened by a powerful hand planted in the softer flesh at the bend of my waist. Instinctively I pulled at the hand, thinking it was there because of a dream or a mistake in identity, but it was clamped down tight as steel. His hand was thin and hairy, like its owner, and had the special strength of the thin and hairy, of the wiry wrist that can hold very tight for brief periods of time. It was a thin, hairy strength in the night, which had, through my drowsiness, the quality of spiders. With a tremendous effort of both arms I pried the hand away, but it snapped back upon me again as if controlled by a spring. He hadn't said a word, nor had he made breathing sounds. We fought a while more, silently, until the hairy vise of his hand went limp. Then we both rolled over and slept, back to back. Or so I thought.

In earliest dawn, when I woke up, he was gone. His wallet and watch still lay on the little lamp table, but his clothes were gone with him. I dressed quickly and walked, drawn by sure knowledge, to the edge of the sea, scrambled down the slope and out along the tar-stained stones to the next head of land and beyond it. The sun had just begun to warm my skin when I saw him sitting small beneath a chalky cliff, his thin arms clasped over his knees. I gave him his watch and wallet and tried to comfort him. I was sorry for him in what he must have felt to be his humiliation, and I had no desire to punish him more than he already had himself. Always through our fierce punishments and our melodramatic humilities I felt — we felt — the possibilities of forgiveness and affection ahead, like inaccessible islands. But they remained inaccessible.

Perhaps the brutality of my victory of strength afterwards

on our bicycle trip from Stratford to Cambridge was not clear to me because of the simple freedom from oppression that it meant. So easy it was on the road, to roll free of his overlordship. Late that afternoon when we arrived in Cambridge, he mentioned with mock modesty to the lady of the local touring house that we guessed we were "pretty tired, ma'am. We left Stratford this morning." She gave a squeal of admiration and went up to draw a bath for each of us, but I gave him only a hostile stare. When he looked boyishly puzzled I flared out in anger that "the humble person doesn't puff himself up" over achievements nor announce them to the first stranger. I felt particularly embittered because of my certainty that with a stronger person I could have gone much farther that day. Perhaps he believed that I had been humiliating him on the road and attacking him at rest to punish him for the Nonnydale night. I don't think I was, but I wasn't fit to judge; neither of us had yet begun to understand the extremities of power over other people that lay within us. Sitting in our separate hot tubs upstairs we stewed privately, steeped in our rich hostilities. We thanked the lady of the house for our baths: yes, we felt refreshed indeed, and we wished her a pleasant evening before we walked off toward dinner, leaving her with that look of surprised approval we had come to expect . . . "Such nice, *courteous* boys! Especially for Americans."

When I knocked on his door the next morning, again he was gone, this time having taken watch, wallet, and bicycle key with him. He did leave a note, though: "I have erred. I have also forgiven. And you . . . ?"

Surprising, how elated I was, cycling alone at first; later, how accustomed; and finally, how bored.

The Song of Lorenzo the Magnificent

Not thinking more than twelve months into the future, we accepted the fellowship money and left for the Mediterranean. Perhaps we believed that our *Wanderjahr* would decide something for us, that by flipping ourselves like coins into Italy we could land with heads up. I felt like a swindler; I had no definite idea of returning to the Fine Arts Department after the year abroad, but then I had no definite idea about anything concerning myself. I knew only that I was growing tired of myself and my world, and I felt that Janet was growing tired of me. She maintained, a little weakly, that she wasn't, but I worked on her until she admitted at least that she *was* pretty tired of hearing me say how tired she was of me. It was in this mood, after sending applications in triplicate to half a dozen institutions, organizations, foundations, and agencies, that we set sail. Our purpose was art history; the year, 1958.

We found Italy greener and more shapely than anything we had ever seen, but we were hardly prepared for the Italians' finding us younger, livelier, and better than we ever remember ourselves to have been. Strange that they should have loved us so openly when we had so much trouble liking ourselves; certainly it had more to do with their capacity for feeling than with what we were. Perhaps they loved us because Janet's hair was blond and my eyes as dark as theirs. Perhaps they loved our love of Italy, at times more articulate than their own, or our fluent Italian, correct, but not too correct. They were amused by our Swedish car and our thick, bouncy shoes. They were even amused by all the money they thought we had, which was a little paradoxical. Ah, money. Janet's family was always trying to give us some, so that I could go to medical school if I wanted, or if not, so that we could enter the Fine Artistic world in style. But I was from a poor background and stubborn; as I once overheard Janet saying to a friend, "You have no idea how unpleasant a person from a poor background can be about it." Clouded was our post-fellowship future.

Still, to the makers of our beds, the servers of our food, to the collectors of our tickets and the chance companions of our walks, we seemed rich and on a perpetual honeymoon. They simply would not believe we had been married almost three years. In our Pensione Speranza in Florence, where we could always be the life of the party by opening our mouths and saying "*basta*" or "*pasta*," we were the only people who did not spend the evening, every evening, hypnotized by the TV set. There was the ceremony of a chuckle all around when we said our "*buona notte*" at nine o'clock to go upstairs and struggle with Michelangelo's sonnets or write encouraging letters to friends who were threatening suicide in Chicago or Vienna. "Aha," the rolypoly cheese salesman would say, "going to bed?" And the cook, not to be outdone, would say, "Aha, going to bed?" We were always *gli sposini* — "the newlyweds" — or *I signori giovani* — "the young folks" — never known by name, followed everywhere by wistful looks. How many times the cheese salesman sighed his bad breath at us (apparently he had to eat all the Gorgonzola he couldn't sell) and said, "America is a young country. Like you. Strong! New!"

For this, Lorenzo the Magnificent was partly at fault. Early in December, excited by our arrival in Florence, nostalgic for the Renaissance, we had memorized his quatrains written for a masque of Bacchus and Ariadne, beginning

> *Quant'è bella giovinezza,*
> *Che si fugge tuttavia*
> *Chi vuol esser lieto sia:*
> *Di doman' non c'è certezza.*

That is: "How beautiful is youth, which escapes us ever. Let him who would be happy be so; there is no certainty of tomorrow." Three glasses of wine, and we could forget about the world ending in a bang or a whimper; a fourth, and we began quoting Lorenzo, feeling fresh, affirmative, proud — a Renaissance lord and lady, we.

The people at the *pensione* were amused to hear us quote their poetry, so we did it too often. Most of them knew some of Lorenzo's song more or less correctly, but they smiled when we began the first line, and they picked it up as if they hadn't dared sing out such verses since school days. However, it did not lead to conversations on the Renaissance; they always turned the meaning back to us: "Ah, yes, how wonderful to be young, to travel, to see beauty, to forget tomorrow." Or they passed through us to images of themselves: "Ah, yes, we too used to dance and sing and quote poetry, but now that time is finished for us." As we smiled our way through one coffee bar after another, treating the major, or his wife, or whoever it was, or being treated by them to dozens of cups of espresso laced against

the winter air with brandy — "corrected coffee," they called
it — their social imagination created what it most needed.
They needed us as a sign that the world was again capable
of rebirth; we came to need their easy explanation of what
we were, since we seemed to have none of our own that was
so desirable.

Numbed by indecisions, pursued by letters that begged
me to be doctor or lawyer, silently accused by Janet of
wanting to become beggar or thief, I would sit with her
amid the cramped, cracked walls of our third-floor room,
listening to the Dacron shirts and panties going "drip-dry,
drip-dry," and I would make up names for our generation.
It was a favorite game of the time. "Unappetizing. Worried.
Never Happy or Good. Old Before Our Time. In Need
of — "

"If you start talking about a moral equivalent for war
again, I'm going to scream."

"The major's wife will love that. She'll think you're
having an orgasm. In the afternoon, yet."

Janet would soften. "Please, darling, you know you always hate yourself after these arguments." (I strongly disliked remarks of that kind; I wanted to hate myself on my
own schedule.) "And you know I don't really care what
you do. It's you who worry about it. I just want you to
decide to do *something*. What does it matter what you do,
anyway, compared with what you are?"

"That's nonsense. You don't know what you are until
you know what you can do."

"I wonder where I've heard that before? Could it have
been yesterday, in this very same room?"

"Noble truths are oft confirmed."

"But you don't know yet what you can do."

"Right."

"Then you don't know what you are."

"Right again."

"You do seem to have a problem."

But it was always up to her to find temporary exits from our impasse. "Paul, let's not completely spoil today because of what's coming. We're free, and in Florence."

"Tall, young, free, and in Florence. You forgot the 'tall' and 'young.'"

"Well, that's what I meant. I won't even ask you about tomorrow, or next month. Or next year. But what would you like to do now?"

"Drip-dry, drip-dry," went the Dacron shirts and panties. Across the alley a fat lady would be hanging up her non-Dacron laundry and singing "Vissi d'Arte," which she sang every afternoon about four o'clock.

Meanwhile, Lorenzo's stanza was becoming our trademark. As we stayed and December grew on, the *pensione* regulars began quoting *"Quant'è bella giovinezza"* right on cue, with our appearance in the living room. It went like one of the themes from *Peter and the Wolf* — one animal, one theme, and ours that carefree song of youth. The theory that we were basically one animal was indeed current. The old major's wife — she was the one especially fond of the "I too used to dance all the time" approach — apparently looked on us as one creature with two hearts; while the major himself, the Speranza's realist, hinted that the beast with two backs was more likely. At any rate, people in the *pensione* seldom spoke of us separately, except to inquire after the other's health. We were one person, plural only grammatically.

I suppose our un-Italian habit of quietly having differences encouraged the notion that we had none. Our admirers never admitted knowing what every linked pair of travelers knows, whether married, related, or merely friends: that a long voyage provides unlimited opportunities for ruining beautiful experiences. Not that all such experiences will be ruined, but each couple will sooner or later devise its own system of delicate cruelties for occasional use. In Florence, I used our morning system. Sunlight on the coffee-stained tablecloth was the setting; then courteous greetings all around; then gulps of coffee served with ordinary bread, butter, and marmalade. We had lived together long enough for me to have learned that, fifteen minutes after her first cup of coffee, Janet is invariably summoned away to the *gabinetto,* the w.c., or whatever its local designation. Thirteen minutes after coffee, therefore, I would introduce some important remarks. Just as I was reaching the moment of essential truth, she would begin to look embarrassed and say that she was terribly sorry, but could I hold on for a minute? I usually doubted whether I could, but she knew she couldn't, so she would bolt away, shamefaced, while I rose politely to my feet. The other breakfasters would smile at me and nod at her pretty back. *"Ecco, la bella* Gianetta goes away."

On one morning I remember well, I was just about to demonstrate how Michelangelo's Slaves, only half emerging from their rough stone at the Academia, could tell us more about ourselves than we had ever learned before when Janet made her uneasy departure. The only other person in the room at the time was the wiry little major. As I stared at the coffee stains, reminding myself that Lorenzo the Magnificent had been succeeded by Piero the Fool, the major walked over to our table, put his sharp hand on my shoulder, and laughed. He always laughed before he spoke, even the night when he described the mutilation of Mussolini.

"Ah," he began, "even the most perfect couple has a few dark moments."

"The most perfect couple — that is, us?"

"But, of course. All of us think so. Wherever you go together, you bring back to people their own happy days."

"Well, it is good to be of service."

"*È come.* Just two nights ago, a friend of mine saw you at Da Zi Rosa having dinner. . . . Oh, I have always wanted to ask you one thing. In Italy we have a saying that professors do not eat beeefsteak, but evidently, for you it is no problem?"

"Well —"

"But, of course, America is a rich country. There, everyone lives better." He turned to go, but I couldn't let him have his favorite parting line that morning.

"Excuse me, Major. I do not remember when I told you that I was a professor, but I must confess that it is not completely — umm — true."

"But *la bella* Gianetta told me."

"Oh, she told you that? How interesting."

"Of course, to us in Italy, it never matters what a person does, but what he is, in his heart. You are *simpatico,* young, with all life ahead of you, like your country. Ah, here comes my wife. She will chat with you. *Arrividerci.* Till this evening."

The major's ample wife greeted me with her favorite look, full of generosity, nostalgia, and self-pity. When she asked what we had planned for the day, I was tempted to say we were going to scour the city in search of ourselves. But I didn't. For one thing, I didn't know the Italian word for "scour." Then Janet returned, and we all began to talk of Fra Angelico.

Still, on most mornings the human resources of the

pensione were devoted to sending us off well. The design for each day of our *soggiorno* was the concern of all, each in his own way. The round-faced waitress who had two little children but no husband would bring the coffee with great good cheer, saying, "This evening — nothing!" She meant, of course, nothing on television worth seeing; but on other days she could report in triumph that *Lascia o Radoppia,* an Italianized *Double or Nothing,* was on, or that *Il Musichiere* was to have that young lawyer from Ancona who knew every popular song ever written. She felt that a clear sense of what evening offered could help us organize the day ahead. The major's wife was likely to remind us of the joys of that time of life when one dances, and that we must gather in the richness of the present day. The young man at the desk had often a new hint about a half-hidden Peruzzi coat of arms over a doorway, which we might find diverting. The cook and the cheese salesman would chatter for a while about the gustatory adventures we could have in certain quarters of town, and so it would be with the others. The newlyweds, *la bella coppia,* would go out among the dark or brilliant streets of morning, braced by the good wishes of all, prepared to feel yet smaller before the great works of the past.

Christmas season in Florence brought the shepherds down from the Tuscan hills to play bagpipes and reedy flutes for the city dwellers' silver coins. In all the little churches, nativity scenes appeared in miniature, graced now by electric lighting and circular tracks on which the Magi and the sheep moved in frozen jolts. But the days grew fierce that winter, and so did our tastes. By tacit agreement we returned day after day to the massive stone men of Michelangelo or to the impassive men of Masaccio in the church of the Carmine; nothing else was strong enough. At the Carmine, we stood transfixed before the images of Saint Peter, the rude, expressionless fisherman, walking among the poor and sick of medieval Florence. In his russet, his green, and his power, we found a healing force, as if his coins were being offered us. And for a while we seemed to be offering in return coins enough to heal the fortunes of the dark church, since one hundred lire had to be put into a box to light the Masaccio chapel for each five minutes or so, and we usually stayed for hours. Through American know-how we discovered, however, that a one-hundred-lire piece could be pushed down into the slot deeply enough to throw the switch and then be retracted for the benefit of young art historians.

As the brilliant lights came on, I would give my best imitation of Janet's uncle, who had once taken us to the Chambord for lunch: "Order the best. The government pays." Janet was not amused. I had developed an uncanny habit of offending. After boring her for years about problems of art and vocation, I would see her deep in thought before *Peter's Calling*, and I would begin to whistle Jimmy Durante's old song, "If Washington needs me I'll answer the call, but they better not call me collect." After which would come a dirty look from her, an irritating smirk from me, her charge that I didn't know what things to take seriously, my charge that her uncle and Jimmy Durante were not things to be so taken, her charge that Masaccio *was*, and if *she* ever dared laugh in the presence of art, I would never let her forget it, all leading to silent rage from her, raging silence from me, and much tapping of fingers and humming over the cutlets and mediocre wine at lunch.

Yet, we would gather golden or graceful moments of Christmas art — Gentile da Fabrianos or Simone Martinis

— to discuss over supper at the *pensione*. We had to present our friends there with something shining to cover the confusion of our days. On Christmas Eve we attended the midnight Mass with them at Santa Croce. The choir, the chamber instruments, the frescoes of Giotto, and the fervor of the older people moved us, but, of course, we did not kneel. When the major, who had been eyeing us constantly, asked us why we hadn't, I answered in a calloused tone that we were not believers. Perhaps this was another of those moments that I hoped, uncomfortably, might lead to a confrontation. The major only wreathed his face in a smile and took our arms. "Ah, my young friends," he said.

The days after Christmas, sometimes rainy, sometimes limpidly mild, Janet and I spent apart. I don't know what she did — I decided not to ask — but I sat in the Palazzo Strozzi library, reading about the burning of Savonarola. When we met on those afternoons to go back to the *pensione*, it was already dark. If we dropped in to visit a favorite corner of the Bargello, we could hardly see the marble saints through the murk, and we felt the coldness of the stone floors at if we were standing on our unsheathed bones. In the streets, the headlights from the little Fiats were piercing and hostile; the fumes from their engines were heavy in the damp air. For us, the ending of the year was hardly a festive time.

The *pensione*, however, surprised us all by serving a genuinely festive New Year's Eve dinner at no extra charge. Every tablecloth was changed. Brilliant whiteness greeted us without the accustomed coffee stains, wine blots, and tomato-sauce driblets. A bottle of deep-red Chianti, the unadulterated *vino nero* of the Tuscan countryside, stood on each table in its straw jacket. After the homemade *fet-*

tucini, we had fish and meat courses, salad, excellent *bel paese* by courtesy of the beaming cheese salesman, little sweetly frosted cakes with Italian flags in them, fruit served in clean bowls, and fresh coffee. We drank reciprocal toasts to the cities of Italy and America:

"To Reggio Calabria!"

"*A* Baltimora!"

"To San Sepolcro!"

"*A* San Francesco, California!"

This went on until we began to feel uneasy about exchanging Jersey City for Perugia and Akron for Verona. There was homey good cheer at all the tables and pride of foster parentage among the Italians as we told droll stories about New Year's Eve in Times Square. Our round-faced waitress asked us to stay for the *pensione*'s own celebration in the living room, where they were going to roll up the carpet, dance to records, and drink wine until everyone fell asleep. We refused politely, saying we had plans.

"I understand," the girl said. "You will be going, then, to the big party at the American Consulate?" And she gave us one of her favorite looks: *You are from the big glittering world, and we are just plain little old us.*

"Yes," I answered, resigned to our importance, "we think we ought to go."

In truth, we hadn't heard that there was a party at the American Consulate. We didn't even know where the American Consulate was. Our plan had been to walk the streets, have a few drinks, feel nostalgic for who knows what, and make a wild resolution or two. It was to be a personal evening, but we could not explain that without sounding boorish. The major's wife gave us her blessing. "It would have given us great pleasure to see you dance, but on such an important night it is better to dance with one's own people."

After a brief discussion of this general truth, we left.

In the streets, there was little celebration. There was, instead, a nagging, wet coldness. We had come too far seeking warmth and significance to accept huddling in doorways as our rite for a holiday eve. Even on the slender tower of the Palazzo Vecchio, the torch flames, orange in the night sky, flickered before the onslaught of wind from the mountains. Out along the Arno, bright lights were playing, but the water, swollen by the recent rains, took on the color of old coffee. In the Piazza Signoria we felt our presence to be singularly unnecessary. Whether from custom or the bitterness of the night air, the Florentines were welcoming the new year "in the family." Under the three great arches of the Loggia dei Lanzi, where Lorenzo had sat to watch masques and pageants five hundred years before, only a few figures passed, muffled against the wind, but warm lamplight shone from the windows of the nearby houses.

We inquired our way to the American Consulate, with the notion of perhaps picking up a crumb of native festivity. After a long walk along the torrential river, we found only a high house built around a courtyard, barred and shuttered. Hearing laughter from some upper window, we hovered about the big door. We decided to go in. We decided not to. Yes, all Americans are supposed to be welcome at these holiday affairs. No, it might be embarrassing. Surely they won't turn us out? Yes. No. Maybe. But. Finally the gleaming policeman on guard looked at us closely, as if he had seen us many times at Communist rallies. He asked us why we were "circulating" near the Consolato

Americano. Janet began to present our case, but I said *scusi* to the guard and pulled her away, again unwilling to explain. As soon as the Consulate was out of sight, Janet stopped short, exuding waves of indignation and hostility.

"You see?"

"See what?"

"It's so humiliating and stupid!" she said.

"What? And don't talk so loud."

"Every petty decision is impossible. God, it's sickening. Should we go in or stay out? Should we go to the Uffizi or the Pitti? Should we go to a movie or write letters? Should we order *pasta* at lunch? Should we go to the American Express now or later? God, all those agonies over nothing!"

"So I'm neurotic. What else are you trying to prove?"

"If you can't make the decisions that count, then every trifle is misery. Can't you see that this could go on forever? You'll crack up someday because you can't decide between chicken salad and a BLT."

"Thank you. Will that be fifteen dollars?"

"But it's just common sense, Paul."

"I thought we agreed a few years ago that the time is out of joint, and common sense is hardly —"

"Oh, your head is out of joint!"

We began to walk very fast back to the center of the town. There, in narrow streets between *palazzi,* we found a series of well-lit bars, each beginning to close as soon as we walked in. Bright lights shut down all around us while we gulped our brandies and exchanged genial, hollow congratulations with men who were dying for us to leave. It was not too much after eleven o'clock when we were again in the cold streets.

Janet shrank within herself against the wet wind. When I tried to comfort her, she pulled away. Her pale hair blew raggedly around her face as she spoke. "Why are we here? Why are we anywhere? Who wants us? What good does it do to reject and reject? Not to live like ordinary people? Why bother reading and thinking and looking at Giotto when all it leaves us with is a holiday like this? Any idiot can enjoy New Year's Eve. But not us."

"But we've had some good times," I said. "Think of some of the places we've seen together."

"And what does it leave us with? Nothing! A stamped passport and sights we'll forget in a year. You won't even take a camera. Just nothing, nothing. God, I'm so lonely and miserable."

"All right, I should have known it all the time!" I flared up. "What you really want is a life just like the one you used to sneer at. Settled like your roommates in a comfortable suburb with comfortable hubby running father's comfortable business. Well, this is a fine time to tell me! I'm not going to do father's business. Or anybody else's business."

"I didn't say that. My God! Maybe I'm just too stupid. It's marvelous. I've tramped all over Europe washing your goddamn underwear so you can tell me I'm selling out to the bourgeoisie."

"Now, wait a minute!"

"You wait a minute. Making great declarations about not going into father's business. Like a college freshman! I can *see* you're not going to do anybody else's business. Do you think I'm completely blind? You're never going to do any business at all. You'll stand in front of Masaccio with your mouth open all your life while I smile sweetly and tell everybody that you're trying to find yourself. Well, I won't go on with that kind of life. I can't stand it! If that makes me an average American housewife, then that's a thousand times better than worrying about nothing but yourself when half the world is starving."

"Oh, I see. The world is starving because I like Masaccio, but comes the revolution and you turn into an average housewife, and then everything will be all right." I noticed that my arms were swinging here and there. "Hunger will be banished from all India! Disease will be no more! Sweetness and light will —"

Janet burst into tears. "Paul, please, please, we can't go on like this. It's all my fault. It's just that it was New Year's Eve and I couldn't help thinking —"

"You couldn't help thinking that you want your tree and your daddy and all the pretty toys. That's your idea of what life is supposed to be. Well, maybe life isn't a nice little game for all the pretty children. Did you ever think of that?"

"Ah, but youth is beautiful," Janet said coldly, staring into space.

"Oh, why don't they take their beauties of youth and stow them in the Palazzo Vecchio?"

We had reached the door of the Pensione Speranza. I suppose we were headed for the privacy and comparative warmth of our room. But a cheer from the living room intercepted us. We had forgotten about the *pensione* party.

Everyone seemed flattered that we had returned in time to contribute our energies to their *piccola serata*. Their party did seem in need of aid. Only one of the three huge flasks of Chianti on the floor had been opened. Beneath the intersection of the two hanging red ribbons, the round-faced waitress danced listlessly with a gentleman who wore amazingly pointed shoes. The TV set, which was being used as the stand for the record player, but had not been turned around, stared at the room with the accusing anger of the unemployed. On a couch to the side, the cook was tapping her feet vigorously enough to "Scusami, Scusami Ancor'," but the major was slumped in his seat while his wife cooed to the cheese salesman and a few invited friends that she was crazy about parties. As soon as we had accepted two brimming glasses of Chianti, the major tried to engage us in a debate on world federalism. Evidently he wanted to take his mind off his weariness of dancing or of the company, but the debate fell somewhat short of brilliance as a distraction. For one thing, we were all in favor; for another, our Italian, among many other skills, was not going very well that night. At last the major turned to us with the bittersweetness of a father to his lovable children and said not to let the old people bore us.

"Dance, dance," he said. "It is your night, the night for dancing."

A chant went up from the gathered public for the young Americans to dance. We refused demurely at first, saying that we had only meant to drop in for a few seconds. "Ah, *come gli sposini sono timidi,*" said the ladies, "they are so shy." The difficulty was really not shyness but fear of a ridiculous showing. It was years since we had danced together. Finally we consented in order not to insult our hosts. They jeered happily at my resigned insistence that I wasn't much of a dancer. Their nostalgia for the antic youth they wanted us to have was irrepressible. It triumphed. Wine was poured around from the second flask; the music was turned up. We danced to "Ti Dirò Che Tu Mi Piaci," the inevitable "Volare," "My Tennessee," "That Old Black Magic," "Tico Tico Ti," and dozens of other Italian and American records. To the slow music we made circles; to the fast music we did the rhumba.

"What wonderful lines she has."

"They never get tired."

"Oh, to be their age again."

Janet was amused by my improvised steps and air of savoir-faire, and her every step melted the old people into joy. The third flask was opened. No one else danced. I put my cheek next to Janet's during our slow circles and found softness there as of ages ago. We became a vision to the people circling close around us; we became for the moment, within our power, what they wanted us to be. When the clock struck midnight, I looked into Janet's wise eyes and said, tentatively, *"Quant'è bella giovinezza."*

Everyone picked up the verse immediately in a cheering, singsong rhythm — the major and his wife, the round-faced waitress, the cook, the cheese salesman, the man who ran the office — all quoting happily as if Lorenzo's words were a traditional New Year's song, like "Auld Lang Syne."

> *How beautiful is youth,*
> *Which escapes us ever.*
> *Let him who would be happy be so;*
> *There is no certainty of tomorrow.*

They crowded close around our dancing bodies, their bodies older but their eager eyes somehow far more youthful than ours, quoting Lorenzo's song, raising wineglasses, hungry for what they saw in us and thought we could give, for youth, strength, glitter, suppleness, and promise.

Out of Moscow!

SUMMER in Moscow that year was sunny and dry, not too hot — good for picnics and boat trips down the river. On the front pages of *Izvestia* Eisenhower and Khrushchev, cheerful as melons, smiled side by side, promising home visits. Already there were lesser visits, exhibits, cultural exchanges; the air was lively with Moscow's enthusiasm for Leonard Bernstein, so young, so vital (New York had already loved the Moiseyev Dancers for leaping so high), while at the American Exhibition in Sokolniki Park peace and friendship were bruited about beneath the August sun. But then the cold wind began early as so often there, blustering through the first week of September, whipping the birches in the parks, raising construction dust from the gutters, roving among the old military walls and onion domes. With summer's end, people along the streets in the wide night seemed fewer and smaller, clutching the tails of their topcoats about their knees, stooping into the wind. Past them, the green trucks roared.

It was the beginning of the theater season. A crowd milled through the unpretentious front of the Art Theater for the year's first performance of Chekhov, and slightly apart stood three people, waiting. The two men — one tall and fifty, gray, a bastion of a man, and the other much younger, shorter, softer, with short hair and round face and horn-rimmed glasses — were jiggling their arms and rubbing their hands from time to time. Their summer suits were too light for this wind. The older man seemed to be in discomfort about his discomfort, concealing it when he could. The younger gave himself wholly to the cold, jiggling and rubbing and even stamping away. The woman, in her plump blondish forties, was snug in fur jacket and gloves: she had been well advised by her travel agent.

They were together strangely. The woman and the young man were from the same leafy neighborhood of a Pennsylvania town, which was proud of the young man for having worked as a guide at the Moscow Exhibition. His article in the *Evening Herald,* "To See Ourselves As Russians See Us," had been much admired. When the woman had arrived a few days earlier (having done the Mediterranean and Eastern Europe), she called the young man (he cursed himself for being the type who always appealed to other people's mothers) to arrange this evening together. The young man doubted whether he could, because it was his last night in Russia and he had planned to see *Three Sisters*, but the woman said, wonderful, they could go together. Her treat. Arranging for tickets in the Information Bureau of the Hotel Ukraine, they had bumped into the older man, also there to make a reservation, and the woman had said, "Well, we're all in the same boat," meaning, at least in part, "We're all American" (the tall gray man, after a hesitation, nodded). She had offered that her Intourist interpreter, the sweetest little thing, pick up all their tickets at the theater just before the play and meet them outside the lobby. A friendly plan, a good plan, except for the bite of the wind, and the reactions she seemed to cause in the two men: boredom in the younger, irritation in the older.

"I'm sure they make wonderful rockets," she was saying gamely, "but the shops *do* have a way to go."

"Quite likely," said the older man. He did not consider the point worth arguing. "You may be interested, on the other hand, to compare tonight's play with, let us say, *Kismet.*" He focused on the distance, above the crowd, and concentrated on self-discipline. To debate with this mindless woman or to let himself jiggle like that boy: either would be a disgrace.

The younger man wondered idly at the International English of the other, but again was distracted, scanning the crowd for someone. Then he felt guilty. Mrs. Bober was being generous, her husband had died that year, and he should be more attentive to her, more interested. One accomplished this with middle-aged mothers by asking after family health. "How's Natey, Mrs. Bober?"

She smiled vaguely. "Oh, we . . . I call him Nathaniel now."

"Well, how's Nathaniel, Mrs. Bober?"

"Very independent, Jerry," she said. "He's on his own, you know." Here her smile was brave.

"He finished Cornell already? That was quick." The young man took to scanning the crowd again.

Mrs. Bober signaled with her brave smile that the tall man would be welcome, too, in the conversation. He did not accept. "Finished? Yes. Well, in a way. You would understand it better. He said he had learned what there was to learn there."

"He must have worked very hard."

"I suppose. Anyway, he's playing the guitar in New York now. And he announces a folk music program on FM. Oh, it's *very* interesting. He's got *lots* of interesting friends."

"I'm sure," said the young man. "Could you tell me what time it is, Mrs. Bober? A Russian friend promised to meet me here. It's my last chance to see him."

She tucked up the wrist of her black glove to peek at an islet of gold. "Ten minutes until curtain time," she said. "My guide should be along now." And indeed she smiled recognition as out of the lobby lights, buffeted by the crowd, came a girl in square jacket over summer dress. "That skin!" said Mrs. Bober, in unilateral conspiracy with the men. "Like fresh cream, and not a bit of makeup. Am I envious!"

The girl's round face truly was made of clear skin, but her eyes seemed tired. "Well, here she is now." Mrs. Bober smiled at her and patted her on the head. "Nadya," she said, "do you know that you're a darling?"

The girl said, "I have obtained the tickets, madam."

"Thank you, dear. I'd like you to meet the rest of my theater party. This is Mr. Volmenin, a new acquaintance, and Gerald Pearl, whom I've known for years."

"Jeremy," the young man muttered.

"Of course," Mrs. Bober said. "Forgetful me."

The older man bowed from his bastion, kissed the girl's proffered hand, and said, in native Russian, smiling calmly, "Accept my sympathies for the time you have lost in accompanying this trivial creature."

The young man, brisk, shook her hand and said, after a pause, also in Russian, "Please forgive this man his lack of courtesy." Mr. Volmenin gave him a brief startled look, then again subsided into his complicated smile (complicated, in that his lips parted, letting out a bit of soul, while his eyes beneath iron-colored brows closed completely, folding his contempt deep within).

"Very pleased," the girl said to both of them, in English.

"Oh, I'm impressed," said Mrs. Bober. "How do they speak?"

"Adequately," the girl answered, and escorted the three into the theater.

"We'll find our places," the young man said to her in Russian. "You run along and do some studying, or whatever you do."

The girl said, "Shall I present the limousine after the play, madam?"

"Do," said Mrs. Bober. "We'll try to whisk the men away for a little party."

The tall gray man said nothing.

The last-minute crowd, fidgety, a trifle baggy, bustled past the photographs in the foyer of earlier three sisters, of Chekhov himself, of Othellos and Inspector-Generals, and carried the Americans down toward their seats in eighth-row center. Tourists had been getting the best seats all summer. Amid the buzz and the straining necks they barely had time to settle themselves — Volmenin's gray-suited shoulders rising above the row of shoulders, Mrs. Bober's gold drop earrings finally hanging motionless and the black silk lining of her fur jacket thrown back to catch the light (a pale blue suit beneath), Jeremy Pearl's face with its owlish glasses thrust forward while his eyes looked elsewhere, inward, backward — when through a sudden hush the seagull on the front curtain rose and all their faces were bathed in white light from the stage. A bright provincial noon, complete in every detail, shone through airy curtains into the guest room, and in the dining room fired the heavy crystal and the candlesticks into fresh glitterings, all in preparation for Irina's name day party. Olga, pensive, put down the notebook she was grading and said, "Father died just a year ago, on this very day, the fifth of May . . ."

Alexander Volmenin let his big shoulders slump. He

sank into the bath of Russian words — warm, poetic, prophetic — flowing to him from his childhood with a clarity as of the world first perceived. (Olga saying now, "I distinctly remember, in the beginning of May, just at this time, everything in Moscow is already flowering, warm, sun-filled . . .") Ah, art could be everything if only, if — But Baron Tusenbach, striding back and forth in his well-pressed lieutenant's uniform, was already in his first speech about the longing for work, and Volmenin's shoulders stiffened again, as he knew they must: ". . . a massive something is moving toward us, a healthy strong storm which is coming, which is already near, and will soon blow away the laziness, the indifference, the prejudice against work, the rotten boredom from our society. I shall work and in twenty-five or thirty years every man will work. Every man!" So. The healthy strong storm. It *had* come, in seventeen years, to be exact, after Tusenbach first spoke that promise. To Petrograd first had come the beautiful purging violence, and he — little Sasha Volmenin — had run away with his family. Better to have died. Ha! Hypocrite, coward, liar, voluptuary — whom could he fool? Himself? He remembered his father shouting into the telephone (how and why did he still know that Blok once had the phone number 612–00?), clatterings in the streets, his mother forcing him to sit in his shuttered room while she read aloud (Krylov's fables in a smelly leather binding, especially "The Frog and Jupiter," he remembered). "Kerensky, Kerensky," they had said at dinners, and so at the age of eight he had found himself in England, at eighteen in California where he would take his degrees. Architect of suburbs and supermarkets. He had done well enough in America. He despised America. Young fools in short haircuts he despised, popular music, pointless mechanical contrivances and, above all, popular music played over mechanical contrivances for the benefit of short-haired fools. After thirty years there, he writhed still to hear the English language mumbled. His own English was perfect (*poy-e-try*, *flaw-tist*) like all his fluencies (lovingly he pronounced: *Le Corbusier, Die Schöne Müllerin*, which, he knew, put other architects at a considerable disadvantage). The pointlessness, the neon inanity, the glut, the aimless flow . . . He despised it — but who had forced him to stay? What gunpoint had kept him at the chamber music, the women who adored his manners, the white table-cloths and good Burgundy in San Francisco? He knew his case — tall aphoristic exile with Flight-from-Revolution tic, Yearning-for-Mother-Russia groan, cherisher of his own symptoms, hungerer for finality. Expert at hypothetical crises, he had persuaded himself not to marry, for "if-he-decided-to-return-to-Russia" could he also answer for a family? Yet he had not decided. Complicated smiler, he had watched himself turn ironic and gray, iron gray. Long hair and eyebrows: gray. Face: turning gray. Suits: gray. Ties: gray. Socks: dark gray wool. Black shoes: now gray from Moscow dust. For with the decisive days over, half his century gone, here he was, finally, with his tourist visa, walking the raw new housing sites, feeling idiotic, feeling driven . . . Two days ago a tableful of Moscow architects, sharp-nosed hounds, had sniffed and barked into his dissatisfactions. They sighed over his elegant Russian and made what they considered subtle remarks about him and history. First, vodka and shoulder clappings: what a canny old fox he had been to sit out the century's troubles in California! Then the solemn faces: but now it is time to work! To work! Bark, bark! The people must be housed. His people, who had suffered much, who spoke his language, who needed

him. Did America need him? And a canny old fox should
know when to join the winning side. He would have high
position, be designing the future ("Stalin no longer . . .
you understand, it is quite different now"). Decide, decide.
Incredibly, he felt himself knowing that they were right.
Stupid, but right. He, always bright, wanted now, with
desperation, not to be wrong . . . Here, Chekhov at the
Art Theater, the seagull on the front curtain rising and
falling, the naturalness, the impeccable diction — this was
to be a taste of the wine and music and softness he would
never stop craving. The rest would be work. But he shifted
uneasily in his seat; the palms of his hands were still tick-
lish from the fur he had eased off the shoulders of this
damned accessible woman next to him. (The sisters were
almost in tears over learning that Colonel Vershinin had
lived on the same street in Moscow — Old Basmanny —
where their girlhood had been spent.) She was a plump little
specimen, reeking of money and widowhood. She was stupid, but she was drawn to him, she was rich; there were
others like her . . . A house in Rome, perhaps . . . Really,
she was, in her way, a rather flighty, delicious little creature
— *canard à l'orange* . . . He squirmed in his seat. The
audience laughed as the fat and aging Doctor Chebutykin
declaimed, "For love alone Nature brought us into this
world."

Florence Bober smiled up at the stage. Her face wore
that emollient beatitude reserved for Good Things, which
had regularly sent her family into a rage. Her husband had
never liked Good Things, not really, and so he had refused
to believe she was truthful in liking them. Her children
now worshiped Good Things, so *they* refused to believe she
was truthful in liking them. This she understood. Many

things she understood, but could she change them? She understood the three sisters through their wistfulness and their clothes — both familiar matters. Her guide, Nadya, had tried to talk her out of the play; that was foolish. Faithfully she had seen the puppet show and the circus, the czars' jeweled eggs and the pictures of the Cossacks riding into battle — the whole silly round for silly tourists, but now she had a warm feeling about Moscow for the first time. The story of the play was so simple, really, and she could so easily read the moods of the sisters: Olga in her blue school-mistress uniform, so responsible and tired and willing to love; Masha still in black, self-dramatizing (Mrs. Bober's doctor had told her to avoid self-dramatizing), anxious; Irina in her white frock, frilly and just right for a turn-of-century spring, and so full of seeking, seeking. Florence Bober might not understand Russian, but she understood the language that clothes speak. Too well . . . Two days ago, her guide had taken her out in the late afternoon to see the new housing going up on the outskirts. (In fact, she remembered first noticing Volmenin there, tall, pacing alone.) She had thrown a fur over her shoulders because a friend in Mellonville had warned her to be prepared any time for the cold breeze in Moscow, but when she stepped, powdered and encased in her fur, out of the Zim limousine, the gleaming door almost bumped a workman who had no shirt on at all. He was wheeling a barrow through the wreckage of construction like a monkey, and his naked upper body was streaked with sweat and yellow dust. She apologized with eyes and hands in a flurry, but he — didn't smile, or spit, or sneer, but simply refused to give any sign that she existed, and pushed on, lips harsh. He stank. People had been stinking near her all summer, in Naples, Athens, Warsaw . . . (Never had she traveled alone before.) She had read their clothes and had seen their eyes read hers, hating and envying. Yes, they wanted what she had — she had only to reach for one of her purses and they went slimy-servile (that was the way her Mellonville friend had put it) — but their hatred reached through her pretty gloves and hats and evening furs to include herself — she knew it — neat and round within. What tranquility did her friends and doctor possibly think she could find traveling alone? . . . Why couldn't she change? Even this handsome nasty Russian emigrant squirming in the next seat saw her as — as what she was: a short woman coated with silliness and fur. But could she change? Who had coated her in silliness and fur so that she would never be able to get out? Who? . . . She knew, but she tried to distract herself with the play again, even picking apart the sounds. Her guide had told her to listen for the words *v Moskvoo, v Moskvoo* — "to Moscow"— which the girls would say so many times, and when Irina finally was standing thin and alone in the middle of the stage (accordion music floating through the window), chanting it over and over — *v Moskvoo!* — Florence Bober began to cry silently. What was she doing in Moscow? Who wanted her? Shouldn't a son be traveling with her, guiding, offering his arm? . . . *Her son,* lost in that awful room in New York, rust rings, gas smell, everything too damp to touch; why is it so *arty* to share your life with cockroaches? "Mother, you are a Philistine," he had said. "A little square female Goliath. Couldn't you just go away? Bleach your hair some more. Do good for the needy. Buy a nice new coat. Have a ball! Just don't bother *me*, okay?" She stole a glance at Jeremy next to her, with his kind moony face and moony half-smile. Why couldn't *he* be more like Jerry Pearl, so studious, so good to his family? She remembered that same butterball face with glasses from years ago

— Harvard hadn't changed him, Russia hadn't changed him; there were still boys who didn't think that decency and love and such things were all phony. And she found herself trying to concentrate on the play but in truth feeling, she knew, terribly sorry for herself, saying silently to the boy next to her, "Be my son, be my son . . ."

Jeremy Pearl stared vaguely at the stage, stunned by the changes Russia had worked in him, which he sensed now might never be undone. At first, despite his annoyance with the general shape of the evening — Borya's failure to show up, Mrs. Bober's wanting from him what he couldn't give, Volmenin's superciliousness — he was reminded how much he loved this play. It was comforting, rewarding, the incarnation of words he knew so well (just that spring he had received an "A" for a senior essay called "Chekhov's *Three Sisters*: The Patterns of Yearning"). Under its spell he could ask himself, rather mildly, what he *would* remember of his Moscow summer. Not the arguments about unemployment, surely. But the girl in Leningrad. The quiet poets, perhaps, eating strawberry jam from spoons, reading aloud to each other night after night lines that history would not yet print, with honest voices, honest eyes, unafraid, owning only a few books and a pencil, arguing about every word, believing they served Russia and all men simply by being true to what they had seen and felt. Borya, behind a screen of cigarette smoke and flying shirttails playing the "Chromatic Fantasy and Fugue" (Borya always behind a screen of some kind) . . . These images were Jeremy's shield, by which he avoided certain things, and the Art Theater's listening rows, the stage glowing with its young actresses in white and blue and black were the perfect final embellishment. But when Irina first raised her arms to the May noon streaming through the curtains, saying, "I don't know why there is such a shining in my soul . . . This morning I suddenly felt joy," he had seen her white hands shrivel in a trick of light, like bacon fried too quickly. So the eeriness began again. He had always been a serious boy. Before coming here he had been serious about reading his Marx and Trotsky and Bertram Wolfe so that he could argue seriously about the competing systems, but nothing had prepared him to see history, wildly, as he did now, as a design for mangling hands. By accident it may have happened (he was, he knew impressionable, disturbed from the first by Moscow's old people, too many of them crippled or sick) that when his turn had come to distribute the red-white-and-blue buttons at the Exhibition entrance — one to be plunked into every outstretched hand — all the old hands shoved in front of his nose seemed to be missing several fingers, or to be somehow gnarled, withered, smashed, or stiffened, or blunted, or ruined. He never saw the faces of that shuffling mob, only the thousand hands outstretched, coming on. Bewildered by the ruined old hands, he had lost all sense of the relevance of arguing against people who had undergone so much brutality (he saw the cocky young people as being lined up by history for their turn to be mangled, he felt his anger released in all directions against the bigshots anywhere who were preparing to let this happen), and it did not seem an accident that the shabby man had risen up against him, of all the guides, during that day's dusk, violating the debate over Ways of Life. "You came to sneer," the man said. "To wave your imbecilic toys in the faces of this gray mass. Look at them — war takes the best, and that's what it leaves." The onlookers stirred in hostility, not against Jeremy but against their own bitter speaker. "Find me one complete man of forty in that mass. Just one who has turned out to be an attractive tall human being . . ." He breathed alcohol in Jeremy's face and the crowd pushed him away, but the guilt had lurched on in the American boy until he began to have visionary experiences, like seeing Irina's tapering fingers wither in the half-century to come. So that when Colonel Vershinin, laughing, spoke his lines of a world in which people like the three sisters will be a majority and "life on earth will be unimaginably beautiful, wondrous," Jeremy Pearl swallowed to keep a stone out of his throat, the intolerable desire for his own unconfessed visions, which he knew could never be: Goodness on this earth, the life of warmth and honesty, the sound of Mozart. There was no place, no promise, no escape. That is what he had tried to tell Borya, in a cliché-deadened way, two days ago. He had felt too guilty toward him (yes, because the boy had suffered) to tell a straight truth. They were walking in Sokolniki Park, not far from the Exhibition, through afternoon air that still rang praises of summer (through the birch groves, the sunlight displaying soft blots on the ground), talking of America and music, Borya with the crinkled half-smiling eyes of the perpetual smoker saying that if he could travel anywhere and could compose anything he wanted, that would be paradise enough for him. Again the false belief that blunted his intelligence: that elsewhere, outside of Russia, there is an idyll of freedom, hence a perfect life. Jeremy, uneasy: "But listen, what does our art in all its freedom say? Can't you see the chaos, the sterility, the disintegration [cliché, cliché, cliché]?"

Borya: "Not important. If art is free to say the truth about its world, that's all you need from it. Ours isn't."

Jeremy: No answer.

Borya: "Anyway, your jazz says to me, 'Life. Energy.' Take

any of the new groups on the Voice — the New Jazz Messengers [chuckle over pronunciation], Horace Silver doing his own compositions . . ."

Jeremy: "I don't know. I don't listen to jazz much, actually."

Borya, with a quizzical look: "And what is this you keep saying about not knowing where to find yourselves? I can locate myself easily. No problem."

Jeremy, edgy: "No problem? What's it like?"

Borya: "You want to know what it's like? I'll tell you. Look, here is home — one room, two rooms, see? [Facing Jeremy, blocking out the spaces with his lean pianist hands, his shirttails flopping out of his trousers, as usual.] Yourself lives there, and your family. That's one thing. Outside — over here — is the State. That's another thing; you want to keep it out, like the weather. Understand? Fine. Then there's the famous knock on the door. Everyone listens; it's the State. The State wants to come in. So your father is gone. Why? Don't know. He was a cellist; maybe he played a piece Ezhov didn't like. But there is still yourself, so you try to find another place, with yourself in, and outside things out. You're not confused about who yourself is; you know the things you love, you want to live . . . Look, you people talk about yourselves like borderless countries, expanding, shrinking, you don't know how far. But there's no joking about where a border runs when it has to be patroled." Borya looked at him straight and simply, his thin face carved by the sunlight. Jeremy had felt ashamed again.

Baron Tusenbach was dead, but old Doctor Chebutykin read his paper, as usual, saying: "It makes no difference. It's all the same."

Olga said, "If only we knew. If only we knew." Down

came the curtain. The play was over. Lights on, strong applause, and the crowd in a burst of conversation moving out past the picture galleries toward vodka, toward tea, toward love, toward sleep. The three Americans were pinned numbly together in the rush. Mrs. Bober had immediately offered her limousine, of course, to take them all back to the Ukraine for drinks or coffee, but the two men from different heights above her head had shaken "no" with only the barest of smiles. Jeremy was anxious to slip away from the older people so that he need not waste precious time and energy introducing them to Borya (if he came), but Mrs. Bober seemed anxious to have company until her car arrived and Volmenin anxious to argue with him about the play, so he was stationed in front of the lobby again, part of the same absurd group, while the street sifted toward emptiness. The wind had grown even stronger, hurtling against them.

". . . art," Mr. Volmenin was saying, "and some concern for truth. Two things not in great demand in America, my boy." He spoke with mild irony, but hoped the stupid child would disagree. He had an appetite for demolishing someone (particularly someone with short hair) before his solitary walk to St. Basil's.

"Chekhov is superb," Jeremy said, "and I'm all for art and truth. But I don't see what it has to do with America." He remembered how weary he was of arguments. Occupational hazard of young American in Moscow.

Mr. Volmenin smiled. "My dear boy. I happen to be an addict of the theater, which gives me ample ground for comparisons. I saw this very play put on in 1955 by your off-Broadway — a movement, by the way, that is naturally parasitic upon European and Russian playwrights. The performance was thin. Thin and sterile." (He said *stair-*

aisle.) "And as for the crude blatancy of your Broadway —"

"Mr. Volmenin," Jeremy said, "you don't really expect me to argue for Broadway against Chekhov, do you? Honestly, now."

"I suppose not." Illegible smile. "I suppose not."

"In fact," said Jeremy, suddenly angry, "let's shuffle the virtues and vices. When will we see Koestler put on here? Why is it that any anti-American play can be put on somewhere at home, and nothing of the kind here?"

Mr. Volmenin raised his eyebrows. "*Any* anti-American play? I doubt that, strongly. *Darkness at Noon,* incidentally, is a minor, dated dramatic work. However, from my conversations with highly placed people here, I can assure you that all worthwhile works will appear in due time."

"Oh, to hell with your highly placed people! You're just the kind of gullible tourist they secretly despise. Do you think any intelligent *real* Russian believes the promises of bureaucrats?" Jeremy experienced one of his rare desires to hit someone in the stomach.

Mr. Volmenin gave again his complicated smile and let his opponent's crudeness reverberate. Equanimity was sufficient proof of rightness. The boy obviously had embittered acquaintances here, probably among the university castoffs. A leading professor had told him of such individuals who relieve their personal inadequacies by infecting the minds of foreigners. Weak-minded foreigners, preferably.

Mrs. Bober tucked herself further into her fur jacket. These men — wasn't there enough conflict already in the world? In addition to which, they were acting like boors toward her. But she always felt it her duty to pour oil on troubled waters. "Oh, *weren't* the settings lovely?" she said, appealing to both of them. "All those country sideboards and curtains, with the sunlight coming through?"

Response: a condescending nod from Volmenin, Jeremy looking in other directions. Well, one last try. "And those actresses — pretty as pictures. So expressive. My guide told me the play was about their frustrated loves and their yearnings for Moscow, and I really could feel it, even without the language, like a wonderful silent movie." Bright look to left and right, pregnant with all her store of amicable comparisons.

"My dear lady." Volmenin said, "the play is sad, but still, it speaks of the eventual triumph of socialism. Which you, if you like, may see around you at this very moment." She looked around, in expectation. Some theater-goers were still walking away, huddled, toward Sverdlov Square. One neon sign shone in the distance above. (It said, "Explain to Children the Rules of Traffic.") "They have all *come* to Moscow, so to speak," said Volmenin. "They have arrived, you see, to begin the era of honest work and useful living that the sisters and Tusenbach were trying to foresee in the play." He was oversimplifying so that she would understand.

"Oh, this is too much," Jeremy said wearily. And to Mrs. Bober, "Your version of the play is better than his, you know. Their yearnings for Moscow really stand for something else, something unfulfillable. It's not a matter of program. The regime hasn't done a thing for human beings like the sisters."

"It has *eliminated* people like the sisters," said Mr. Volmenin. "For their own good it has changed them, given them something to do. They were bored with their pretty clothes and houses — well and good, the government has taken them away. If it is humanity you are disturbed about, young man, you may rest easy. It is all slowly working out for the better."

"Thank you," Jeremy said. "That's very soothing." He must have heard a cue, for he launched a set speech. He had been feeling a bit ironic, he said, about humanity after Colonel Vershinin's last lines — about men having outlived battles and wars, which left a big empty place to fill. It was interesting to see how well that place had in fact been filled since 1900, how well it was all working out. He became too excited, stopped.

Mr. Volmenin still spoke calmly. "If you will remember, Vershinin concludes those remarks — by the way, you are not pronouncing his name correctly; the letter *shah* never takes a soft vowel. In any case, he finishes with the specific wish that love of work be combined with education, and vice versa. I can only observe that his wish is being heeded in the Soviet Union, and not in America." He turned away, in cool disgust.

But Jeremy argued into the middle of his back. "I'm sorry. You have to see things in a certain way — white here, black there — for reasons of your own. I don't know what they are. But don't imagine they have anything to do with truth as it is."

Volmenin turned to him again, very gray, very tall, very tired. "And how, if I may ask, is truth?"

"Complicated," said Jeremy.

"Ah, I congratulate you. You have a word that saves you from decisions. How convenient. Is something good or bad, you are asked — is it right or wrong? And you will answer, 'complicated.'"

Each turned away now, Jeremy kicking a little stone, thinking: He's right, damn it to hell; and Volmenin: Even a young fool can penetrate my motives.

(A taxicab rattled down the empty street. Now Jeremy was sure he had somehow offended Borya. Where was he?)

Mrs. Bober was torn, feeling her mission to be universal sympathy, but seeing Jeremy hurt and confused she settled for home loyalties. She said, "You know, I could actually understand the girls when they said, 'To Moscow.' How does it go, dear?" She put her gloved hand on Jeremy's sleeve. "Oh yes, *v Moskvoo.* I was so proud of myself. I didn't need the words. You're quite right. Those lovely creatures stuck away in the provinces, like dying flowers, wanting something they could never have. But the settings *were* lovely." The last was a gesture toward total appeasement.

Jeremy nodded vaguely, but he was not paying attention. Probably, he didn't deserve the friendship of a person like Borya. If Borya didn't come in five minutes, he would leave, whether or not Mrs. Whosis's limousine had come for her. Let Volmenin wait — he seemed to have the hots for her anyway, if that was possible.

The three stood, restless in the wind, tall, medium-sized, and short.

"It's not the wind, not the wind that bends the branch." Borya Leontiev walked angrily through Sverdlov Square, into the wind, with his shirt flapping, singing to himself one of the many folk songs that he hated. It was a favorite trick, when he was fed up. Without fail, it made him feel worse. Fed up, fed up, and a thumb-sized loudspeaker installed in his head to bring him his people's music. Long live autonomous popular culture! He had taken special delight in walking all the way tonight, making the American wait, reading aloud as he crossed Herzen and Gorky streets all the printings in red and green against the night sky. "Citizens," he announced loudly, "Put Your Money in a Savings Institution! Peace to the World! See the Films on Moscow's Screens! Taxis Will Deliver You to Any Address with the Greatest Convenience! Glory to the Party! Citizens!" (People stopped to listen.) "Do Not Step in Front of Moving Vehicles — Wait Until They Have Passed!" (People shrugged, and walked on.) All the idiot signs he had read, but then he decided to Reason with Himself: "It is windy tonight, Boris Davidovich. You were a sloth all summer, so now you're afraid you'll never be a great composer. *She* is leaving; you were nothing to her but an interesting experience. You are getting thinner, you forgot your coat. That's why you feel bad." So he had tucked in the tails of his wilted brown shirt, as if that would help against the wind. But it's not the wind, "not the wind that bends the branch. It's just the shaking of my heart" (accompanied by a thousand autonomous balalaikas playing in unison). But it *was* the wind. He smelled an ending in the wind. The night was acrid with it. Summer was over, the lovely, airy, false summer, floating on wine and friendship, falling in love with a girl who wouldn't have looked at him if she were Russian, talking of Bach with American friends, weaving daydreams with them about going to Italy, to Paris, to New York, and there composing a new cosmopolitan music — he and Stravinsky and Bernstein and Horace Silver: Les Quatres. "Boris Davidovich, you are an ass," he said. Boris, son of David. How could he have allowed himself in Sokolniki two days ago to speak to Jeremy of his father? As if twenty years of self-discipline had taught him nothing, years of watching quietly while certain friends exposed themselves for nothing, years of watching coldly while the others loved their leaders loudly and were dandy Pioneers and took engineering degrees and feathered their nests . . . Nauseating, to have dissolved in self-pity because summer was ending and he had met some Americans with big sympathetic eyes. Now his life was another piece of political evidence for Jeremy. Adaptable for the *New York Times*. So convenient . . . Borya rounded the corner and saw in a swatch of light Jeremy still waiting by the theater door, with two other foreigners. Of course, of course, he should have known. ("I want you to meet this *interesting* young Russian. They killed his father. He's a musician.") God damn them all anyway, taking control of their lives, flying off, waving their green passports, full of projects, complaining about spiritual unfulfillment, forgetting him in a month, a day! Not giving a damn that he would spend his life as a piano teacher for the youth of Yakutsk if he was careful enough to show no spirit at all, and if not . . . ?

Borya walked up to Jeremy in the swatch of light and briskly shook his hand, without apologizing. "I have brought you a farewell present. Don't forget us." He held out in his palm a red mechanical pencil and an address booklet with alphabetical tabs. On the blue plastic cover of the booklet there was impressed a *sputnik* whizzing among blue plastic stars. Volmenin, looking down, was touched by Borya's chiseled, ascetic face and floppy hair — the true young Russian intellectual — and by his gift. There were a thousand such small forgotten things about Russian life that he had so missed. Ah, sentimentalist. Melancholist. But it was for young men like this one that he would build.

Jeremy introduced Borya to the two older people (Volmenin shaking the thin hand fervently, flooding the air with Russian expressions of pleasure, his eyes lit with gray fires, while Borya said to Mrs. Bober, *"Khau-doo-yoo-doo."*) Poor Jeremy was confused: by his friend's brusqueness, and by the miniature Kremlin tower imbedded in a glass bubble at the pencil's midpoint, with a miniature red star atop. He stared at the absurd objects and at the tension of the hand that held them out. He never seemed to keep pace with Borya's sense of ironies.

Volmenin (Lordly Conciliator) patted Jeremy stiffly on the shoulder and said, "Perhaps you would be pleased to know, my boy, that you have received a traditional Russian farewell gift. Why, in the play we just saw, as you know, of course" — he had turned to Borya and shifted smoothly into Russian — "young Fedotik makes the same presentation to the schoolmaster."

Borya glanced at the tall emigrant whose Russian was still perfect. "Oh yes," he said. "Of course. How coincidental." He already had a fresh cigarette in his mouth. Volmenin wanted to light it for him, but Borya was quicker, with the souvenir Zippo Jeremy had given him blazing from his hand. "Your *Zee-po* is wonderful in the wind," he said to Jeremy and to Mrs. Bober, who, seeing that he was pleased about something, was pleased. Borya's face as it flickered in the yellow light, the thin compression of his lips about the cigarette, the strange Russian words, were all out of some wonderful movie.

"Now that we're all together," she said, "couldn't we have a little party somewhere?" And she rested her hand on Jeremy's arm. (He wished these people would stop stroking him, so that he could escape gracefully with Borya.) "Your friend will come, and Nadya, too, of course. We would make the nicest international family around a table."

"Splendid idea," said Volmenin, throwing down his dead match. "You are indeed a hospitable soul. The cafe above the Moskva would be perfect." He beamed at Jeremy, Mrs. Bober and Borya: warm, warmer, warmest.

Jeremy looked at Borya through his solemn glasses, and the Russian boy thought, Jeremy wants to talk to me about life and art tonight. It would give him great emotional satisfaction and leave me a total wreck. If I'm not already.

"*Do* ask your friend, Jerry," urged Mrs. Bober.

"Yes, do indeed," said Volmenin.

"What does the furry lady want?" Borya asked Jeremy, wtih a sweet ironic smile. Volmenin, too, smiled a discreet complicity in the epithet.

Jeremy said, in dismay, "She wants us to go to the Moskva for a drink or something. But I thought . . ."

"That would be very nice," said Borya. "I'd love to go." He smiled his lean smile at Mrs. Bober and said, "*Zahnk-yoo.*"

"Then you'll go without me!" Jeremy burst out, in Russian.

And Volmenin, in Russian: "I shall be pleased to serve as interpreter. And we shall have Nadya. So" — to Jeremy — "don't feel too pressed to join us, if you have other plans."

Mrs. Bober, hearing the word "Nadya," said, "Where is that girl? Oh, will she charm *you,* Jerry. But I promised your mother I'd keep you out of the clutches of Slavic beauties."

In Russian Jeremy beseeched (and beseeched himself not to be plaintive), "But Borya, I hoped we could talk . . . alone . . . it's the last chance. About the play. About a lot of things."

Borya let smoke blow across his face. "You know, Jeremy, one gets tired of Chekhov. Let's just — "

Jeremy turned and stamped off, into the windy night.

Mrs. Bober was stunned. "Where is he going? Jeremy!"

she began to call down the street. "Where *are* you going? *Jeremy!*"

Volmenin was saying to Borya, "I'm glad we shall have this chance to talk. I've not had the good fortune, until this moment, to meet any intelligent young people here." (Arch-manipulator, preparing to hint that they go off to chat, with no Americans present at all).

Borya looked after round dwindling Jeremy, felt a pang of affection, another pang of loss (these last two days had had nothing else), but suppressed them as well as he could.

And Volmenin, continuing, " . . . the rest of my days here, to work, to help. A subject of some importance to me, naturally. And to you perhaps not without interest."

It is irrational to resent all émigrés, thought Borya. I myself or my father might have gone, if we could have. He tried to manage a courteous look toward the gray one who was droning on about himself. "Perhaps some other time," Borya said. "I'm at the conservatory. Leontiev." And without another word or gesture, he, too, was gone.

Mrs. Bober, standing forgotten in her fur jacket, had let her smile turn a bit wan. (I *wish* all these boys would let me know where they are going.) But then she caught the glare of panic in Volmenin's gray eyes. That glare was something she happened to know about; it had to do with abandonment. She didn't know what he and the Russian boy had said to each other, but this lonely arctic man was in trouble. That much she understood.

Volmenin turned toward the glow of Mrs. Bober's compassion: the most beautiful glow in the world. (Ah, orphaned Sasha! (Yearner for *maman!*) He felt a desire for the warmth of her fur jacket, for her furs to warm him in this windy world. No! No! He turned again, without a word, in the direction Borya had taken. That boy was the future. He would follow him, expose himself, apologize for his arrogance, somewhere in the cold wind. He would humble himself until the boy told him what he had to know.

The huge limousine was there with Nadya holding the door open, much distraught about being late. That boor of a driver had made a pass at her. "Sit next to me, dear," said Mrs. Bober, making herself small and round as she climbed in, "and tell me about Russian men."

But Volmenin was bending, looking in through the limousine door, gray hair falling to his cheeks, saying, "Fair Mrs. Bober, may I still accept your offer of transportation for this aging body?"

"Oh, please do." But that made it sound as if she agreed that he was aging. "Please *do*," she said again, to solve the problem.

"You won't mind if I call you Dulcinea?" he asked as they drove off.

"Why in the world should I mind?" She knew the reference, of course, but only from the Sunday crossword puzzles. There were so many Good Things she had not yet gotten around to.

To Nadya, it was a great relief that the tourists would be accompanying each other.

Driving toward Okhotny Ryad, they passed Borya, walking alone and bent into the wind, his shirt flapping, cigarette aglow. Tomorrow, thought Alexander Volmenin, I, inquirer into destiny, will find young Leontiev at the conservatory and we shall discuss art, and Russia's future. Tomorrow night I shall walk, solitary meditator, to St. Basil's. There I shall decide.

Since girlhood, Florence Bober had liked men who cast an aroma of cool lotion even hours after shaving.

Out in the wind, Borya passed a telegraph office, an ice cream shop, a government shoe repair station, a forty-five-kopek gas water stand — all closed. He passed the monument of Iury Dolgoruky, founder of Moscow, in his helmet, on his horse, and he said to himself, Curse the monument of Iury Dolgoruky, founder of Moscow, in his helmet, on his horse. He decided as he walked to curse all the monuments he could think of. Curse the Pushkin monument. Curse the Lenin monument. Curse the Mayakovsky, Gogol, Herzen, Ogarev, Lomonosov, Minin-Pozharsky, Zhukovsky, Ostrovsky, Gorky, Griboedov, Dzerzhinsky monuments. Curse the monument to the heroes of 1812. He passed the entrance to the Okhotny Ryad metro stop and remembered to curse the monuments in the metro. Curse the stone heroes with submachine guns, the ceramic soccer players, the mosaic peasant dancers. He looked up across Revolutionary Square — so few people out tonight — and decided again to Reason with Himself and in the future not to smoke so much, when he saw Jeremy Pearl (round head down, hands shoved in pockets) almost get hit by a taxicab in a scream of its brakes and the glow of the little green bulb signifying that it was free. Borya hid behind a shadowy poster announcing the Czechoslovakian Glass Exhibition to watch Jeremy shrug his shoulders, ignore the driver's bellows, and walk on toward Red Square and St. Basil's eccentric domes without having pulled hands from pockets. Borya felt a wave of sympathy. No one to talk to about Chekhov except himself. Poor Jeremy. Then: Tonight he will think tragic thoughts. Tomorrow he will fly out of Moscow for New York. Ah, let them all go, let them go —

the rich ladies and the émigrés and the earnest students. Out of Moscow. Boris Davidovich, take control of yourself, take control, don't be a fool. But he heard himself half laughing, half sobbing, speaking it aloud against the night sky: "Out of Moscow! Out of Moscow!"

On the Edge of Arcadia

I T was April, and they were driving across Greece in a Fiat, two young Americans, a sculptor and a poet, both fellowship-winners. They had come from Rome and they were on their way to Athens. Rounding a curve through the silver of Peloponnesian spring, they abruptly came upon an array of fabrics in strips along the roadside, all the colors of autumn and of fire waving in the wind. They saw shawls, blankets, saddlebags, crude tapestries — red, burnt-orange, mustard bordered with scarlet — all, beyond suspicion, the work of hands native to this valley, as the sculptor immediately knew, bellowed, in fact — *Holy Christ!* — and sitting by that clothesline of raging splendors, an old man. His face, as they flashed by in the sun, seemed carved, Sophoclean. Behind him, there was a hint of whitewashed walls, a suggestion of chickens; then it was gone.

On they drove, but not far. The poet's forehead almost went through the windshield as the sculptor slammed on the brakes.

"That's it!" announced the sculptor. "That is the work of the human hand! See how it comes out of nowhere? Like a storm. A vision!" He banged the heel of his hand against his head, and in general made hectic and meaningful tableaux.

They were stopped near two mountains and three goats. With the ignition off, they could hear beneath the wind downhill water — springs, brooks, streams that had still been snow when these travelers had left Rome. Above them to left and right, then falling continuously below, the world curved and coiled in fields of young wheat, olives, pale grasses: a shifting play of green and silver down into the sun, dotted here and there with a bent black crone.

"That's what we've come for, Rick," said the sculptor.

"That's what *you've* come for, Slugger."

The sculptor gave back an ominous look. His face was, curiously, his family's face, of southern California money, sunburnt and bellicose beneath sandy thatch. With a slight twist of his soul, Slugger could have been at this moment sounding off in a locker room instead of seeking the work of the human hand in the Peloponnesus. The thought of that possible twist in his soul could drive him mad.

He launched into an effusion, and Rick disconnected his eardrums, letting his mind sail out upon that landscape for which his nostalgia was lately getting out of control. He wanted to dive face first into that young wheat, to let his body soak into the curve of a hill, to hear passing bells, wind, the plodding of beasts, never again to write a prize-winning ode On Reading a Letter from Alice James to Her Brother Henry in Mount Auburn Cemetery During Warbler Migration, never again to be bright, cocky, irreligious, ambitious, indifferent, shallow, all the things he felt himself, somewhat unfairly, to be.

"— good look at his *face?*" Slugger was asking, with dangerously accelerating veneration.

"The old man's face?" said Rick.

"Well, yeah. What did you think?"

Rick said, cautiously, that the old man's face, what he had glimpsed of it, seemed good, patient, handsome.

"Ricky, it was a work of art! Carved out of stone. Nothing

extra. No fat, no cowardice, no greed. Just that pride, that dignity these people have."

It was an obsession of Slugger's.

The only people left in the world with natural dignity were the Greeks and the Spaniards. And that, only in the deep countryside. He had recently discovered the Spanish Civil War, and spent half a year constructing a towering bronze, *To the Spanish Dead*. Now he was sketching faces, bent bodies, coiled landscapes toward another mountain of bronze, *To the Greek Living*.

"Why do you think he had all that stuff hanging out there?"

"Maybe for the world to see. Leaves, bright feathers . . . I doubt they're for sale."

Rick was not in the mood to bargain with another penniless octogenarian.

"What do you say?" asked Slugger, already shifting into reverse.

Rick laughed bleakly as the Fiat lurched backward. It was a chance in a lifetime, they just *had* to talk to that old prince (that is, Rick had to talk to him: his Greek was primitive; Slugger's, nonexistent), they had to see what the hands around here could still make (which was, of course, Slugger's major obsession: soon there was going to be nothing in the world made by human hands). What they had found in Greece so far were cynical imitations, which could almost fool Rick but not Slugger. He had fumed and raged through Delphi, Arakhova, Olympia, Sparti; only in one or two villages hanging under the bleak eaves of Arcadia did he begin to see what he needed: through dark doorways to shops where the mountainfolk came to haggle, crude magnificence hanging from wooden pegs. But he was a hard bargainer, although Rick, whose preference was always to overpay with a winning smile, had to do the talking. Not to bargain hard, according to Slugger, was to let real Mediterranean people down. To pay too much, to tip too easily, was to sap their dignity — that priceless treasure — in return for a handful of filthy pennies. He was sick of Europe pimping and grimacing and scraping and lying for money — worse than America; in Rome, where he had been sculpting that year, worst of all — and he had worked himself into a frenzy of premeditated reverence for the Greeks as the last MEN in Europe, natural princes every one, at least in the mountains, who could not be bought off, who had pride, whom Hemingway would still have admired, with the result that he squeezed every last drachma, in the name of Greek dignity, until it howled.

This was a strange turn, for Slugger by nature was almost imbecilically generous, the despair of his wife and his gallery, giving away work, sketches, Mexican treasures to anyone he cared for (a numberless horde), while Rick himself, that gusher of alms along the road ("Take. Eat. This is my body, this is my blood, this is a thirty per cent tip.") was a skinflint among his own, never committing a semicolon to paper without payment on the spot, inscribing his name large in books he lent to his mother . . . By now, they were both a mess about money. Slugger had refused to be driven above two dollars in one Arcadian haggling, when the equivalent of three would have brought him a peasant masterpiece unobtainable anywhere else in the world, and could only nod his head, grim and huge, while Rick tore the marginal thirty drachmas into shreds and threw them out the car window, to float a thousand feet down upon flocks and poppies: a curious rain. Rick was then put in charge and emerged — yesterday — from the shop of a blatant old tourist-trapper in Nauplion bearing a rug and a smile. Slugger took one look, characterized the rug as "machine-made" and the smile as "shit-eating." The rug had cost twenty-five dollars, which was as nothing compared to the cost of the smile, payment exacted by sculptor from poet, but today was another day, at least for Slugger . . .

Upon seeing the same car approach twice on the same afternoon, this time backwards, the old man bestirred himself.

Slugger was bulky, Rick lean, the old man taller than either of them and his posture straight as an archaic charioteer's as he held his arms forward. "Young men," he said. "Welcome, young men."

Slugger nudged Rick, who said, "Good day to you, sir," in Greek, clumsily, smiling in self-deprecation.

"*Sir*," chuckled the old man and gestured them toward his place.

Then he chuckled again — "*Sir!*" — delighted with his private reflections. His jacket and trousers, both black, were frayed into shininess, his shirt was open at the throat, letting tufts of white hair escape, which also sprouted from his ears; and his neck, cheekbones, forehead, chin were spare — thongs and bones and print of wind: nothing excessive, as Slugger had said, except perhaps the venerable vagueness of his eyes, which Rick might have called a trifle overdone. On his pure white shock of hair, the country cap sat so high that the sun, from behind, blazed into an aureole for it to float upon.

Slugger was beside himself.

"Sir," Rick began again, and then joined in the chuckle for reasons that escaped him.

Both young men pointed to the brilliance of the weavings

as their explanation. Seen at close hand, the colors and patterns were less startling, not so pyrotechnical, but deep, domestic, strong . . .

"Beautiful," the poet said. "We saw. On the road. Beautiful work."

"Yes, indeed it is. Family work. We have fine hands in the family." The old man held his hands up into the sunlight with grave emaciated fingers spread as if they were the loom, to which Slugger responded with such nods and convulsions of empathy that one of the hands came down to pat him on the shoulder. Men of hands. Toilers, carvers, builders. They understood each other.

There was a pause.

Domestic beasts cackled and groaned. The birds of spring held forth. Beyond, the earth fell away in grains, groves, and ravines. The sculptor nudged the poet.

"You sell?" Rick said, his face abysmal with tact.

"I sell?" repeated the old man.

They nodded.

"Because, we buy," said Rick.

"You buy?"

Nods.

"I sell, you buy?"

Nods.

The old man burst into laughter. He still had his teeth, not all of them rotted. The cords of his throat quaked, until his wheezes subsided into an apology. Now he patted both of them on the shoulders, saying, no, no, he did not sell, but asking, courteously, whether the young men were not, perhaps, Americans?

"Yes."

He pointed to himself. *"Woo-stir."*

"Woo-stir?"

"Woo-stir, Mass." His English clipped them like a sniper's shot. "I been there twelve years, boys."

They laughed uneasily while the old man wheezed again into the face of the sun. "Oh yeah, boys. I left in 'thirteen. Right before the big war, over here. Whaddya think of that?"

"Fifty years ago," the poet said.

"Oh, yeah. Fifty-one years I been sittin' here."

Through gaps in the gorgeous fabrics, they peeked at the family's hamlet. There was a medlar pear tree and a thick dark table against the limed wall, yards scratched and meager; beyond, a mountain slope scrolled part way up with green, flecked at the top with ice.

"Nice stuff, huh?" The old man extended a Sophoclean arm toward the fabrics. "Skirts, *clotes,* bags —"

"Clotes?" Rick repeated.

Slugger, quiet and serious, said that it was more than nice stuff. It was the best, strongest, most alive work of this kind they had seen anywhere in Greece.

The old man took down one of the smaller shawls, and a bag, and settling into his straight chair that faced the road, spread them across his lap. The sun beat fully into his eyes, and upon that splash of colors in his lap.

Rick said that he knew some girls at Bennington who would sell their souls, if any, for that one bag.

Smiling, the old man accepted the compliment.

Slugger was bent over the weaves, tracing out the patterns across the rough wool with his fingertips. There were subdued diamonds of blue and brown that he hadn't noticed from a distance. And staggered borders of black, crosses of dark green running through and around the scarlet stridencies, transforming mere stridency into brilliance, as he explained to Rick, who listened with half an ear.

But the old man nodded gravely as Slugger held forth, then asked whether he, in America, was a weaver.

Slugger laughed when he said no, patted their host on the crown of his country cap, called him "old-timer," all of which pleased the old man immensely. Again he pointed to his chest.

"I weave," he said.

"You wove these?"

"No, no. In *Woo-stir,* boys. Mill hand. Then I started doin' fine . . . Then I got poor."

There was a silence.

"Oh yeah, boys. Bad luck. I'll tell ya . . ." He shook his head. "Bad luck," he said again, this time in Greek.

Silence again. All three shook their heads.

The sun beat down on the empty road; the weavings fluttered.

Rick finally produced the oration he had been rehearsing for the past five minutes: Sir did not sell these things. Now they understood. But a thing they did not understand. Why the things were out under the sun? For the world? To see?

The old man crinkled his eyes, staring slyly up at Rick. Then he beckoned him closer, poured a flood of Greek and an ancient mustiness into his face. Rick grinned foolishly, shook his head, until the monolog began to end with fragments about his not trying any longer to pretend (the old man joyfully wagging a finger at him), he should admit it, he was a Greek boy, or at least of Greek parents. Rick, whose hair was pitch black, whose face was lean and olive, protested, shook his head again with a smile, started to say something in broken Greek again, which set the old man off into yet happier circles, embellishing his totally incomprehensible arguments. It began to be clear that there were eavesdroppers somewhere behind the arras, for whose benefit, partly, the old man was building his delicious scene.

"What's he saying?" asked Slugger.

"I haven't the foggiest," said Rick, playing the Englishman abroad.

The old man turned to Slugger. "Come on," he said, with another finger wag. "Your friend. He's a Greek fella. Right?"

"Everybody seems to think so," said Slugger. "Same thing in Italy."

"Also in China," Rick said.

Now the old man was in splendid spirits, but Slugger was growing ominous, with his arms hanging at his sides. ("Banter," he had been known to say, "is not my line.") He raised his right arm, in which the muscles played, but noticing the attentiveness with which the old man eyed it, grew embarrassed and nodded his head instead toward the weavings. "I was wondering why you have all this fantastic stuff out here."

"Funny you should ask that," said Rick.

And the old man told them. There was a girl in the family — his young niece. It was long time for her to marry. But where can boys be found around here? In the village, they all went away, at least all the good ones, just as he himself had once left. Now they had a boy coming to see, from the north. This boy ("A suitor?" Rick interposed. "That's it," said the old man.) — this boy would come to see what the family had to offer. First he would look at all the family's things (the old man leaned forward, lowered his voice: now they were three Americans in mockery of the Old World). He would count the sheep. He would look at the teeth of the horse. He would feel the chairs. He would ask what the . . . thing was that they could give him. ("Dowry," Rick interposed again, and Slugger nudged him to shut up.) But, this family was poor. Their only treasure was the weavings the women had done. Beautiful work, as the boys said. Fine family work. So, that is what they could give, and it was out in the air today to make it fresh. Then if the boy liked the sheep, the horse, and the shawls, he would say, "Okay. Where's the girl?"

The old man called out, peremptorily, and from a few steps away a woman appeared. "That's her," he said to Slugger and Rick.

She was in the compulsory black, with apron and kerchief and heavy socks. Her face, pleasant but perhaps too strong — almost masculine — was already lined. The Americans bowed, and she smiled shyly, with powerful teeth.

The old man ordered her to withdraw, then called another order to her back.

"So that's it, boys. She's twenty-four, see?" He peered for a reaction, which they did not give. "My wife's brother's son's daughter," he said, looking questioningly at Rick.

"Grandniece."

"That's it. If she gets married this time, that's nice. Up north, it's nice. If no, then you see those ladies out in the fields? Thirty, forty years workin' on the ground, then under it."

There were the makings of another silence. But a Mercedes passed and they could have talked about war or German tourists if the grandniece had not reappeared, carrying a tray with a bottle of white wine and tumblers instead of the expected Turkish coffee.

"Like *retsina*?" the old man asked, and nodded toward

his kaleidoscopic lap, where the woman carefully placed her tray. She began to remonstrate with him — pointing to the wine and the weavings — but he waved her away.

She paused, to look at them. *"Amerikaniki?"*

Rick answered that they were.

"Good," she said, very slowly, as if for children — "Good!" — gesturing toward them and to her great-uncle and back again, giggling. The old man again raised his hand, and in a flurry of affirmation, she was gone.

Three brimming glasses were ready. The old man held his high to admire the sun pouring through in an amber shaft, illuminating the mists of sediment that swirled faintly before his eyes. He asked, half apologetically, whether they knew Greek wine, which was very strong and had the taste of the resin . . .

"We know. We like it."

They toasted each other's health, and drank. The young men had thirsts from the road, eliciting a wheeze from the elder. "Hey! We're not in *Woo-stir*, boys. Here we don't do like that. Insult, if the glass gets empty. Here."

Again they studied the wine motes in their tumblers. The Americans were free to move about in the light, whereas the old man was imprisoned in his chair, beneath shawls and tray, with the sun blazing into his face, probing every crevice in its hide, and surely, said Slugger (beginning to move his chair about), hurting his eyes. The old man waved him off. It seemed that he preferred trying to outstare the sun and he wanted them in front of him so that they could talk.

Slugger had now begun to study the old man's face with bald intensity. The victim was half amused, half puzzled. He adjusted his cap, held his refilled glass up into the sun again, and peeked around to see whether the fixed stare was still upon him. It was.

Rick laughed. "My friend wants to make a portrait of your head."

"Picture? Sure. Got a camera, boys?"

"No, no. He's a sculptor."

"Sculptor?" The old man smiled, in docile incomprehension.

He and Rick had made a game of the gaps in his English. The young man molded the air with his hands. "You know, you know. Sculptor . . . *glyptos!*"

"Oh. *Glyptos, glyptos.* Sure. But what you wanna make *my* face for, boys?"

Slugger was already at work with charcoal pencil and sketchpad. "You're a very beautiful old man."

"Thank you."

"Hold still, now."

"Okay," said the subject, very happy.

Afraid to move, he pointed to the wine tumblers, which Rick made to brim again.

Now there was not a silence among them, but a moment of justified quiet. Slugger's pencil scratched back and forth while he murmured occasionally those soothing words that good portraitists and doctors know: ". . . good . . . that's fine . . . just hold that . . . just a bit more . . . there . . ." Rick was free to prowl about, savoring the spell of spring and *retsina,* studying rocks and fabrics, medlar pears and mountains. He chased a few chickens, stared at rapacious silhouettes (eagles? vultures?) that wheeled against the sun, exchanged cynical glances with the goat, and waved to the grandniece, who smiled blindingly and disappeared, seeming to leave her teeth behind. He wandered back to the road, admiring his friend's crouched concentration and wondering again that nature made provision for such present rage and potential cruelty to be expended through the point of a pencil or into the hammer's head that beat on bronze. They had taken this trip on the urging of Slugger's wife, who said he was growing "completely impossible" cooped up in Rome. All the bronzes that he cast out of his private agony had recently fetched "handsome prices" at a New York show. The danger that he might wax rich and famous was apparently rousing his demon. So he and Rick ("you're his only sane friend") had jumped from rock to rock, from an archaic smile to a golden lion, watched the sun rise from the walls of Mycenae and watched it set through the doors of a Byzantine chapel secluded amid its collection of cypresses, frescoes, hawks, sea, and clouds; and they had haggled over crafts, and now the great forearm instead of threatening a wife was sketching a relic. Rick himself studied the time-ravaged face now as it tipped up toward the sun that had burned it into leather and bleached its eyes. He looked at it carefully, for the first time, and then at its version on the sketchpad; and he grew troubled.

"You've made him look like one of my grandfathers," Rick said to the sculptor. "It's uncanny."

Slugger grunted.

"He does look a little like my grandfather. The thin one." And, turning to the old man, "You look like my grandfather."

"Where?" the old man said, smiling pleasantly. "Your grandfather?"

"Look *like*. You resemble him. Same face, except for the sunburn."

"Same face? No kidding."

("Hold it now . . . just a little bit more . . .")

"You know," Rick said, "he came from a village. Probably like yours."

"No kidding. Greek fella?"

"No, no, no. Don't start that again. From . . . Slavic country. But he told me there were hills, and chickens."

"Yeah? Well, that's it. That's what we got."

(". . . last couple of lines here . . . don't move around too much, now . . .")

Rick was excited. "You know, he came as a mill hand, too. My grandfather. A weaver. It's strange, the same story, but —"

"Bad luck?" The old man, eager, turned to Rick. "He got bad luck, too?"

"No . . . No. As a matter of fact, he had good luck."

Silence, except for the pencil's rasp.

"He had very good luck. He made money, had a big family, got through depressions, wars —"

"*I* made money, boys!"

Slugger threw down his pencil, in disgust at talk, as the old man tried to pitch himself up from the chair but managed only to spill the wine bottle. Only a few drops were left. All three watched the blots swell on blazing crimson.

"*I made money!*" the old man repeated.

He sat back, first closing, then covering his veined eyes. Slugger seemed abruptly anxious to go, Rick not.

"Business. I was a kid. Your age. Her age. Doin' fine."

Silence. Slugger, pacing.

The old man uncovered his eyes — vague, errant eyes. "What's he do now?"

"He?" Rick said. "Oh. He's dead. Dead for six years."

The old man said he was sorry.

"No. He had good luck. Things worked out well for him."

"Mill hand."

"*Started* as a mill hand. Like yourself. He bought some looms. Eventually he did very well, in ladies' blouses. House in town, house in Maine. 'Just like the czar,' he used to say. 'Summer Palace, Winter Palace . . .' "

The old man had ceased listening. He turned toward Slugger. "Luck. We had the store. I — work in factory, work in store. I'm the one, speak English for the family. Money. I want to come back here. Fight the Turks, see my mother. On a ship."

"What happened?" said Slugger.

"Lost it."

"What do you mean, lost it?"

"Lost it," said the old man, and lapsed into vagueness.

Slugger lay his sketch — his blueprint of the old man's physical dignity — on the tray, with a phrase meant to cover offerings, sympathies, and farewell. But Rick said, quietly, "What was it like, in Worcester?"

And the old man astounded them with a prose poem. With fragments, solecisms, and waning breath he composed a 1900 town of great singularity, where the snow was always filthy as it lay, and the gray winter wind never ceased to howl, where a thousand city horses reeked in disease and confinement, and people, pinched by work, grew mean, while the racket of the factories hung everywhere on their heads. He told them how he wrote back, and later people wrote back to him, of the golden land where everything was fine, and it was a lie.

Suddenly his eyes were unveiled and his face, amid its creases, was intelligent.

Then he kicked at a clump of poppies at his feet, and the hairs seemed to resprout from his ears. "Boys," he said, "I'm poor."

They still said nothing.

"Poor. Nothing. I got nothing. See?"

He did not pull out his pockets to wave emptily in the breeze as other men might, but held his palms forward for the Americans to see, one for the sculptor and one for the poet. He held them gracelessly before him, angling his fingers sharply downward to make the cords in his papery old wrists extrude and strain, and the Americans had time to observe that his palms, those blighted contour maps, were indeed empty, while his eyes, as occluded now as any Worcester winter, watched them.

So they were held for another long moment.

The poet cleared his throat, made tragic murmurs. The sculptor shuffled his feet. Eyes watched from a window. Goats rang their neck bells. Then the old man let his hands drop. "Yeah, that's it, boys. That's the way it is."

"I'm sorry," the poet said. "It's a terrible thing."

"Fifty years. Fifty years I been poor."

"Terrible," said the sculptor.

"Nothing here," the old man announced, waving at the medlar pear tree. "Hills and chickens. That's right. That's what we got. But he got the luck. Better man."

"*Luckier* man," said Rick. "That's not the same thing."

"Luck," the old man said, staring down the valley. "He could give to his family. That's what I wanted. That's what's good."

"Now look, old-timer." Slugger took a solid grip of the old man's shoulder — that compilation of matchsticks. "His grandfather got into all kinds of tax brackets selling underwear. Huzzah for him. But did he ever take a boat back to fight the Turks? He never lived out here where the gods used to live. Spent his life in a place like Worcester, you haven't missed a thing. He never saw these mountains, these eagles. He probably never found out what a good day's work feels like in the sun. And you've worked." Slugger turned over one of the hands and tapped its ancient callouses. "You can't kid me, about 'sitting here.' You've worked. You've seen the lambs, the new wheat, every year. Every year. Just look at this stuff around you." He pointed again at the waving fabrics. "You're alive. He's dead. You're drinking wine in your own place in the sun. He's dead six years. So I'm not so sure who's luckier."

(Lies, thought Rick. You're damn well sure this old fossil is luckier, because he slipped out of the clutches of the Industrial Monster. That's your only and absolute standard.)

The old man was quiet for a moment, while spring with wheat fragrance, birds, drifting silver clouds, outdid itself. The road was still, except for a horse cart three bends below, and there was not a sound that Homer might not have heard.

"He's dead for six years," said the old man, and then with great dignity: "I'm poor for fifty."

Slugger smote himself on the brow.

Hearty thanks were offered — in two languages — for the wine, and praise — in one — for the excellence of this family's skills. The old man stepped fragilely along toward the Fiat, disregarding thanks and praise. A knot of women, varied in sizes, but all in black, materialized to watch from a distance, behind the abandoned chair and against the weavings.

For a chance to speak English to fine boys, for the "real fine picture," the old man was grateful. He asked where they were going (Athens), and where after that (back to Rome), and where they had been (Paris, Istanbul, San

Francisco, and so forth), and he pointed to himself, then to the hamlet with its beasts and fruit trees, saying there was the place *he* was going to, today, and tomorrow, and also where he had come from, and where he was highly likely to go the day after tomorrow.

"Poor," he said.

He had the young men pinned now against the side of the car. To let the door open outward they would have had to push him aside.

It was as if he were enamored of the word itself. He tapped both their arms and again intoned it.

"Poor."

Slugger and Rick eyed each other. Their friendship was not deep, but its silent vocabulary could easily meet the challenge of a verb: *Give?* and a noun: *money?*

Give money?

Slugger's southern California face clouded over.

"Wait," the old man said.

He hobbled off impulsively to his chair, picked up the woven bag, then put it down and picked up the shawl instead, and returned with it to the Americans, who watched him and each other.

The old man stepped up to them, holding forth the shawl, which glowed, and looked straight into their eyes. His own eyes made their bleared demand in silence, while the sun again seemed to carve his face, casting shadows in the depths below his cheekbones, blazing on the white hair that escaped beneath his cap and on the ravages of his brow and the harsh stubble that sprouted about his chin and neck.

Now they could give, thought Rick. They could give easily and they knew it. And they knew they wanted to give, each in his own style: that was the right and generous and

American thing to do (CARE packages and United Fund thermometers danced in his head). But poor Slugger's notions of manliness, dignity, pride still existing in a few rocky corners of the earth — in proximity, at least, to certain museums and archaeological sites — that there were still men who wanted simply to be accepted as men and who would not be bought. And what would their five or ten dollars do for this man (surely they were not going to give him more)? Would they change the conditions of his life? Were they going to give equal amounts, in all fairness, to all the old men in the Peloponnesus? Wasn't it merely to relieve themselves of a bad moment that they would plunk their bribe into his ruined old palm? To let themselves off the hook so that they could enjoy their *taverna* in Athens tonight? But it was so easy to give, if that's what he wanted. There he was, waiting in the sun: Still Life with Shawl. So easy, if it would give him a sweeter week or two. How many did he have left? And probably he was corrupted, by Worcester. For half a century he had been a Sophoclean decoration for this roadside while through his head America was still spinning (time-is-money-what's-in-it-for-me-got-to-look-out-for-yourself, boys). A wedding gift for the grandniece. Tactful. A fat price for the shawl. Was that what he was angling for, after all? A bargaining, slightly elaborate with pathos? Right on the Athens road, how many tourist cars per week, all looking for handmade genuine, and sensitive to deprivation at fifty per cent above the market price. But if Slugger were right — that all he wanted was a human ear once or twice in his dwindling life, a chance at the mysterious consolation of singing one's sorrow in broken English to someone who listens and is gone, an exchange of hospitable wine for nothing but the blessing of talk . . . ?

The sculptor had already accepted the shawl, clasped the

proffered old hand, exchanged a forthright *vale,* and was in the car by the time Rick had drawn out his wallet and selected nine bills fresh from American Express — four hundred and fifty drachmas, about fifteen dollars. These he placed in the old man's left hand while he shook the right one (strong, but twig-dry), saying, "Good-by. Here's a bit of luck from my grandpa." It came out badly. The old man said nothing, merely letting the bills lie in his upturned old claw, staring vaguely at Rick's shoulder. The poet's face burned, as he slammed the door.

The Fiat roared off.

Slugger was too choked with rage to speak. Rick saw with astonishment that tears had welled up in his friend's eyes.

Then his own forehead was almost grazing the windshield again. They screeched, stalled.

Slugger had hold of the back of his head — sweat-hot grip — and forced him to look back through the rear window.

"Look. Dammit, look!"

Rick saw the old man with his back turned to them, reduced by distance, framed against the upland groves, his white hair catching the sun as he walked, stiffly. The sun was slanted enough to give each step its illuminated puff of dust, until he had passed through the crimson weavings, leaving his chair behind.

They stared at each other wordlessly. Then Slugger released his grip of Rick's neck and looked instead at his own palm, as if examining it for loathsome contagion.

The poet settled down to difficult thoughts as Slugger reached for the starter. The engine picked up its spark, gas was fed, and they were in motion again — backwards.

"Slugger . . ." Rick said.

But he was talking to his friend's neck and shoulders,

which strained for rearward vision, while the voice, mingling with the engine's whine, muttered out the window something about, ". . . nobility . . . apologize . . ."

"Pay attention now, Slugger. How about calling an end to this farce?"

But they had reached the scene of the crime, against the undulant curtainings. Engine, off.

Slugger leaped out. He slammed the door so hard that the Fiat quivered on its springs. Then he was standing, triumphant, in the middle of the road, looking down at a handful of crumpled bills.

"That noble old bastard," he said, shaking his head. "That's what he thinks of your money. That noble old bastard!"

Rick waited.

"All right, friend," called the sculptor, too stridently for this mild valley. "Pick it up!"

"What do you mean, pick it up?"

"You heard me," Slugger said. "The money. Get out, right now, and *pick it up.*"

"I believe you're trying to sound like Marlon Brando," Rick said.

Slugger bolted back to the car. His face had blotched with anger.

"You going to do it on your own?"

Rick searched his friend's eyes for some sign of a human being. "No."

And Slugger grappled him from the car, pulling Rick's right arm with both hands. Rick was not so heavy as his friend, but neither was he afraid to fight him. He was simply unable to suspend disbelief. Slugger had his arm twisted up behind him now, and half dragged, half pushed him to the middle of the road, where lay the lethal clump of bills.

"Pick 'em up, Rick, and the farce is over."

"No."

Now the arm was twisted up almost to his head. It began to interest Rick to know whether or not the sculptor was actually willing to break a friend's arm in the name of an idea, but then the pain grew amazing and he was being pushed down also by a heavy wet hand on the scruff of his neck. Slugger was forcing his face down into the little pile of paper as an enraged master will push a dog's nose into its own filth, to teach it. That is, to break it. The comparison interested Rick as he smelled the oil and dust of the road, but then the choice was simply to let his arm crack or to swing a wild left back into his friend's crotch or to pick up the money.

He picked up the money.

After they had driven downwards for a while through the valley, where spring was silver-green and the branches threw laceworks of racing shadows, Slugger said, "I'm sorry, Rick."

The poet concentrated on light and shade, olive trees and rock.

"What I mean to say is, I'm sorry up to a point. I apologize for my bad behavior. You do the same."

Rick looked back steadily. "I don't recall any bad behavior on my part."

The sculptor bristled: "God*damn* me for trying to smooth things out! You haven't learned a damn thing from this, have you? About human dignity, about —"

"Yes," Rick said, "as a matter of fact, I have."

Something in his tone finally quieted the sculptor. He looked through the windshield and down the road toward the next stage of his pilgrimage.

The poet opened his fist, where lay the fifty-drachma bills, much crushed and wadded — three of them, to be exact: which were all, apparently, that had dropped from the old man's hand, or that he had chosen to throw down.

Then Rick closed his fist again.